HORIZON

THE LOST PLANETS

DEREK J TELLING

Copyright © 2020 Derek Telling

Original cover design by Nicola Latham
Nicky.D.Latham@gmail.com

CONTENTS

1: DARKNESS

The Darkness found them again, fugitives running and hiding through the valley full of shadows, the river lit by the moon, a ribbon of light. All the wild creatures in the forest are still and silent watching the red dragons. The night is bright and clear as they hover over areas of the trees searching, flying slowly down the valley, looking into the woodland with their sharp eyes trying to pierce its shady places. A large patrol of Protectors is also in the area with them, spread out, stalking slowly through the landscape determined to drive out the escapees.

As the inhabitants of the forest watched the search of the valley begin, they saw one of the hunted, a giant with dark green skin dissolve into the river, becoming a long fish swimming darkly away beneath its deep waters. His elder brother, also tall but very thin, cloaked himself in the shades of the night, the shadows of the moon, becoming still in the trees, lost in the leaves and hollows of the woodlands. Suppressed anger and rage barely kept under control ticked away inside this one.

Several weary hours later the captain of the Protectors gathers the searchers together to say,

'We have been thorough, yet there appears to be no sign to say that either of them has come this way. Perhaps they have split up. The orders given to us all is to hunt night and day giving them little time to rest. It is urgent that they are found, so we will move on and complete another area before we are relieved and can return to camp.'

All the searchers are gone by the time the birds begin their morning chorus, the dawn's first light creeping into the forest. The two escapees cautiously come together in the trees to look out across the river. The hooded one cloaked in black looks at his younger brother to hiss with anger for the umpteenth time,

'They were weak in the end, stupid, they lost it all. We could have helped them more yet they would not let us. Those fools who wanted to rule named themselves Interventionists, the so-called magicians, mad scientists, self-styled warlords, all of them clever but flawed.'

Again, his brother wearily gives him the same reply,

'I told you that you frightened them. You were too intense Brother. They thought you would master them when each one secretly wanted to be the Ruler.'

'Our mother Grendalia would have cursed them. She was the greatest black witch of all,' the Hooded One answered. 'She gave us all her knowledge, showing us how to feel the black joy. I offered it to them. Under my influence it would have been a different outcome.'

The giant shifts his great body and shrugs his massive shoulders,

'You were always mother's favourite until the red dragon Ironjaw killed her. This war was useful, we honed our knowledge and many died because of us. Now the war is lost so we need to escape this place and be gone.'

There is a deep sigh from inside the cowl as the elder one remembers Grendalia whispering in his ear, her words of infernal ambition for his future. They gnaw at his very being, making him crave the mantle of a supreme dark influence and the blackest majesty.

'What is this?'

He points a bony finger at a shadow coming towards them.

The Darkness rising in the morning light is flowing across the water. Warily the two of them watch it's swirling as it comes closer, unfolding as it approaches. It grows around them.

'You look a little lost my friends,' it whispers like a quiet breath in their ear. 'Perhaps we might help each other, I could be of service.'

'Who are you? What is it you think you can do for us?' they ask.

There is a pause, a silence that stretches on as the Darkness retreats to wind itself low around the trees, only to come back, rising high as though it might engulf the two brothers. Its power is pulling at them. Through its dark shades the voice comes again, a sighing echo inside their heads, flattering them,

'I am your talisman, your greatest admirer and I set you free. I have watched your talents being ignored and wasted for a long time. I hid you from your guards so you could escape.'

'So, it was you who made the day suddenly grow dim and the breeze become gale force allowing us to slip away. A powerful piece of magic indeed,' the voice growls inside the cowl, now extremely interested in this formless being.

'Of course, it was me,' the Dark One seems to shiver, its voice becoming a hiss of excitement. 'If you let me help you, I will open many doors and teach you the words you need to be bathed in the darkest magic. I will help you to restore yourselves quickly, then if you learn well you will have the power you crave, the black joy you seek.'

'How long will it take?' The elder brother asks, his eyes gleaming and greedy.

The Darkness suddenly becomes manic; it swirls and dances, rising and falling, flowing away then rushing back.

'You will need great patience,' the Formless One's hypnotic voice whispers, fawning around him. 'We will hide close to them, invade them without their knowing. The Council of the Wise is now in the ascendancy so we will wait, the opportunity will come, and we will defeat them all when we are ready. You will become the Master of Chaos, while I will be your servant in the coming fight.'

The Darkness grows further, expanding, enveloping some of the trees, and it takes them, as they begin to feel the touch of a dark ecstasy, a tincture of the black joy it promises.

A journey of hate and destruction has begun which over the years attracts sinister disciples to their dark mantra. Now, a quarter of a century later they are almost ready to strike, to destroy the centre of those standing in their way.

2: WILLOW

'I am Willow the singer of songs that lull dragons to sleep, the Mouse, the Protector, the glowing light.'

Over and over the girl lying on the bed of straw repeats the words in her mind. Her eyes are open, staring, although they see nothing except the piercing blue eyes of another who comes into her dreaming time after time. His voice is soft and insistent saying,

'You belong with me. Your so-called friends have already forgotten you, they only care about the children of Ambrose. You are lost and alone now. I will not desert you; I will always be there bringing you the black joy and power. We all wait for you and we have great patience. Come with me I will show you the way. Come with me.'

In her head she hears the words. Music, rhythmic and repetitive plays like a church organ, rising to a crescendo before the fierce pain bursts in on her mind, breaking down her barriers. It comes in waves, one upon the other to flood her memories, her hopes and dreams, washing yet more of them away. Suddenly it recedes like a tide flowing back to the skyline, only to return louder than ever, always with that insistent voice urging her to surrender.

'I am Willow the singer of songs that lull dragons to sleep, the Mouse, the Protector, the glowing light.'

She hears the laughter that mocks her, that haunts her, as the words and music come at her again and again, the sharp blue eyes watching for her to fall.

'Come with me. Come with me. Let go, what is past is done. Be one of us. All will be well; we will light the dark passages together, find the great treasures of knowledge and power. Remember they care only for Lottie and Jack; you are forgotten now. Walk with me and when the fire comes to consume them you will be safe.'

The voice stays low, but it is relentless, growing in her head as the music rises again to a crescendo.

'Willow come with me. Come with me.'

Willow screams.

3: THE WOLF IN THE CITY

It is 3 a.m. in the morning. The mist is rolling up the River Avon, following the tide on its way into Bristol on a cold February night. Drifting on through the wide gorge it starts to envelope the Suspension Bridge, shrouding the hundreds of small lights shining out into the night sky.

The Great Grey Wolf is standing above the bridge on a wide ledge, a viewing point which also accommodates a park bench. His eyes are keen, yellow and grey, ears pricked up as the breeze ruffles his fur. It is cold but he doesn't feel it as he watches for his enemy who will surely come again one day soon. Regularly in the early hours, the Wolf glides unseen through the shadowy streets and on to the wide green expanse of the Downs, watching diligently, ready should the Darkness rise again. He knows it will come flowing secretly, silently, transporting itself ready for the fight to recommence.

The mist continues to eddy around him, attaching droplets of water to his fur. Eventually, he shakes himself off and lopes up the track towards the acres of flat green grass, moving like a grey ghost through the bushes and scattered trees. Suddenly he stops, becoming completely still as his eyes flicker and flare, nostrils sniffing the air. Turning his head slowly, ears forward, all his senses are in alarm mode. There is the slightest of movements. He feels rather than hears the danger, something has joined him in the chilly night. He is being watched and tracked.

Suddenly he takes off, running full speed through the flowing mist and dank undergrowth, a long grey shadow rounding the trees. He quickly reaches a place where the path comes out on a level and clear area of the Downs. He goes to ground, becoming ultra-still merging with the long grass, eyes glittering, waiting patiently.

The minutes tick by. On the main road the ghostly streetlights peer through the mist, a police car with lights flashing zooms by. A group of student revelers from a late-night party, noisily sing out of tune pop anthems on their way home to a hall of residence. The Great Grey Wolf becomes aware that there is a deeper shadow, someone is gliding along the dark path. Silently, slowly, a figure appears out of the mist and stops at the perimeter of the trees to look carefully around.

A youth of medium height wearing a cap, a dark bomber jacket, scarf, jeans and leather boots is standing there. The Grey Wolf creeps imperceptibly forward inch by inch, gradually getting closer, although it is hard to make out the features of his face until the young man's head turns towards him. He is wearing an eye patch.

After a short while, the humankind shrugs his shoulders and almost jauntily, despite a noticeable slight limp, swings down the path towards the tree lined main road. The Wolf follows in a wide circle keeping low, getting quite close to his quarry who seems unaware of his presence. Then comes the muted sound of a powerful engine as a chauffeur driven black limousine pulls into the curb. A rear door opens and as he steps inside, the grey watcher hears an excited,

'I saw the Wolf tonight Mother.'

A cultured, soft voice says,

'Oh, well done my son.'

The door shuts on any further conversation and the car drives away, picking up speed until it is lost in the mist.

The Great Grey Wolf watches the disappearing vehicle then turns to lope purposefully across the dark Downs to the other side, going down into the 'Village' and its empty roads. Melting into the shadows when a late-night car passes, he makes his way to stop beneath a huge oak tree opposite Christchurch, its tall spire lost to the mist. A wary fox stops its nighttime rambling to watch from the church wall. It sees a shimmering out of focus movement as the Wolf fades away, to be replaced by a young man in his late teens with a shock of fair hair, dressed in jeans and a warm jacket.

Jack crosses the road and walks quickly towards several Georgian terraced streets; turning into one of them, Maida Terrace, he heads for No 5 towards the other end of the road. The terrace is long with a raised pavement and large stepping-stones up to it; this helped people in past times to get in and out of horse drawn carriages. Opposite the houses is a well-tended, long communal garden full of different sorts of trees and shrubs, from which, on occasion, a tawny owl emits its evocative hooting.

As Jack hurries along the terrace, he notices a figure who is carrying a narrow leather bag over his shoulder, leaning on one of the pillars at the entrance to his home. Another taller humankind slips out of the mist to join him. Jack slows to approach warily, not able to see exactly who they are.

'Well,' says one to the other, 'not the best welcome I have ever had.'

'Spellman!' Whispers Jack loudly. 'You're back.'

'He is indeed,' says the other one.

'Rodrigo, I am glad to see you both.'

Spellman the warrior, who carries the Dragon

Sword and wears its ring, his black face grinning in the streetlight, Rodrigo the wise councilor, Protector, brother of Ambrose, clasp hands with Jack happy to be together again.

Six months has passed since they fought in the mountains and valleys of Andalucia, secretly fighting the evil Magda Cross, the Darkness, Cravenclaw the black dragon and their monstrous friends.

Jack opens the door and ushers them into the hallway; Spellman's grinning face grows serious.

'Bad news Brother, we have lost Willow, she has been taken.'

Stunned, Jack's face pales and freezes. He was eagerly looking forward to seeing the brave young Protector again.

'How did that happen? I thought she had left to follow you to the Spider Planet,' Jack says. 'My sister will be devastated to hear this news.'

'And so are you,' Rodrigo is thinking to himself, watching the shock and emotion momentarily obvious on Jack's face.

'I thought she had stayed around on Earth, safe with you and Rodrigo.' Spellman, Willow's guardian gently replies, 'I wasn't aware she was missing until the fighting on Umorgo stopped. We immediately started looking for her, trying to find traces of where she may have been hidden but we have found nothing yet.'

Jack gathers himself together to say, his voice low,

'You think she is still alive?

'I have to believe she is,' the Black Warrior replies. 'They would surely leave us a body, just to cause us pain and upset if she were dead. However, they seem to like prolonging the agony for the victim and for those looking for them.'

Jack nods his head feeling the anger beginning to rise in him,

'I have bad news too. I am sure we are being watched.'

They both look at him sharply.

'Then we certainly need to hear about that,' Rodrigo replies, then pauses. 'There is also someone else here who will want to listen to what you have to say.'

As he finishes speaking, there is a soft footfall on the pavement outside the open doorway, making Jack spin around to look out again onto the misty terrace.

A shadowy shape begins to form. A woman steps out into the streetlight. She is tall with short black hair, her eyes underlined with kohl and wearing heavy round silver earrings. A long narrow rucksack like Spellman's hangs over the shoulder of her heavy cloak. Her boots make little noise as she moves gracefully towards them.

'I think you may have need of my services, so as always my brothers, you call and I am here.'

Rodrigo says,

'Jack meet Branca, Protector, wise teacher, Shield Maiden and our greatest friend.'

Jack attempts to shake her hand but she clasps him by the shoulders to look directly at him; they begin to smile at each other.

'Oh, I think you'll do nicely,' she says giving him a hug.

'First test passed then,' grins Spellman. 'Is there any food and drink for thirsty travellers?

While the others settle themselves in the large kitchen, Jack goes to wake Sebastian and Lillian. Rodrigo turns to Branca to explain,

'It seems such a short time ago we spirited the twins away from their birthplace before they were even a year old,' he says. 'It was extremely dangerous for them to stay in Horizon, especially with their father and mother gone. We all agreed to Sebastian's genius plan, to have Lottie and Jack hidden from their enemies in plain sight on Earth. I watched them from a distance, living normally as a family with him and Lillian, growing up happily and unusually close, even for twins. Then when we had to tell them who they were much sooner than planned, I saw how that very closeness helped make them even more resilient. Relying on each other helped them with the shock when they learnt they were in such grave danger, which changed their lives almost beyond recognition.'

Branca and Spellman look at each other and she says,

'They will need that resilience again now, there is no doubt our enemies gather. The fight will come again. We will all need to be strong.' Her dark eyes flash and spark, ready for the battle.

4: ROCK OF AGES

On the lost planet of Langamar millions of light years from Earth, in the vast and undiscovered galaxy of Horizon, a tall black cloaked humanoid is communing with his ally. His name is Typhon, the eldest brother, who since he first met the Darkness has learnt well the secrets of the blackest magic. Unbeknown to the twins and their Protectors, he is their arch enemy who has gained an aura that is wholly sinister. An aura that brings the power to command black dragons, that urges his nightmare disciples to follow his malevolent pathways.

'You did well to steal the girl and give her to the demon to change,' Typhon says, his face hidden in his large hood, his putrid breath staining the air. 'We will make good use of her once her spirit is broken.'

Around him swirls the Darkness, the dangerous, undefined rogue energy that flows through the Universe like a river of evil.

'As you commanded Master, I have also sent our enemies a sharp reminder of how frail they really are. We shall soon have the chaos you seek and through it we gain the power to rule all,' the Darkness whispers, fawning around the humanoid, playing the servant.

The cloaked being lets out a sigh of satisfaction,

'I am told the two siblings continue to try to seek out and rescue their birth parents. Well, let them try we will be waiting for them. I have both Ambrose and Rhea safely and separately hidden, their powers taken away. They will never meet again or escape to rise up and thwart our intentions as they once did. As for their children, we will destroy both brother and sister before they grow to their destiny and become ever more dangerous to us.'

The Darkness murmurs softly,

'Yes, it seems that the bond between them is extraordinary; somehow their difference from the planet-bound children of Earth was kept well hidden. Now, it is ever more obvious that they already begin to demonstrate exceptional powers for ones so young.'

Typhon laughs, it is harsh and guttural,

'That may be, but we will catch them however unusual they are, then I will enjoy letting the parents watch the destruction of their children. It will prove our power to all the inhabitants of Horizon, when Ambrose, their one-time hero is beaten and destroyed. With the Council of the

Wise annihilated and his family and friends dead, all will turn to us to lead them out of chaos.'

Replying, the Darkness's voice is a hollow echo, ebbing and flowing,

'After Magda Cross found them everything changed, they cannot hide away now. Even as we speak, she is drawing near again to both brother and sister, watching them, ready to draw them into her net. Although they managed to avoid capture last year, nothing will save them from you now. Our time approaches.'

The Master of Chaos strides out of the cavern. The air moves, shimmering as he changes to rise to full height, a huge statement against the twilight sky. He raises his arms wide, opening his fists, fire burns in his palms.

'You shall all know me soon,' he calls out to the teeming Universe. His voice rises to a crescendo, his rotten breath a fetid wind across the white landscape. 'I will not hide for much longer; you will know me well as you look into the mirror and there I will be. You will know me, and I will release you to do my will.'

Cavorting madly around this creature, the Darkness whispers and hisses its devotion saying,

'I have called our friends to action, even your brother has woken to hear my voice. As I said, one of those who has heard me calling is closing in on some of the twin's allies, ready to do its deadly work.'

The Hooded One bows his head in acknow-ledgement,

'And we will still continue to work in secret right in their midst, until we are ready to declare ourselves openly and strike at their heart.'

The air shifts and moves and he is gone.

The Darkness flows slowly around for a while, communing with itself,

'He has done well since I found him and his lazy brother Gorkus, who it seems is content for him to be the leader, keeping from view in his watery element. With my help, Typhon rises greedily to fulfill his ambitions and I will bind all the dark ones to us,' the Formless One muses. 'He is now growing beyond my control, sinking deeper into his craving for a dark supremacy, it consumes him.

'One day soon he will have the absolute power to restore to me, that which centuries ago was taken away. For so long I have been denied the ability to change shape and have substance, to move among the humankind unnoticed when I wish to. We will see who the Master is then, when the brothers come to know who I really am, and find they are partly my invention.'

The dark shadow shivers and is gone.

On Earth, the black limousine enters a valley in the Mendip Hills; driving up the winding road it pulls into a lay-by opposite the famous Rock of Ages. In this rocky cleft five hundred years before, the preacher Augustus Toplady found shelter from a raging storm, an experience that led him to write the now famous hymn. The fissure stands damp and cold in the mist which clings to the steep slopes of the valley. The car's engine remains quietly running.

Waiting patiently, the lady occupant becomes gradually aware that a shadowy figure is making his way slowly down the rock-strewn slope towards them. Dressed in a cloak and hood and carrying a staff, he has by his side a large black mastiff also carefully picking its way through the boulders. The back window of the car, where the youth sleeps soundly, slides down as the creature approaches and the woman with the cultured voice leans forward to speak,

'Well Naptha, how does your work go? Has she crossed over?'

The creature pushes back his hood slightly to reveal a completely white, skull like face, with a black star tattooed in the centre of his forehead and a goatee beard. When he opens his mouth to speak, his incisor teeth stick out like a vampire's and his brilliant blue eyes glitter.

'She is stubborn but we will prevail,' comes the low, quiet voice.

'I am sure you will not wish to fail us. Our

Master would be very unhappy.'

The Demon's face glows red for a moment and his blues eyes flare at the softly spoken threat.

'Oh, I don't think that is at all possible.'

'Good. We will need to move her soon, be ready. She will be the bait; she will draw them out.'

Naptha's head bows slightly as the window swishes shut and the powerful car begins to move forward gathering speed to disappear around a bend. Silence descends as the Demon clicks his fingers and the dog, which had settled down a little way off comes to heel. Slowly scanning the sides of the valley Naptha sees nothing that worries him, so moving swiftly they scale the rocks and are quickly lost from sight.

A few minutes tick by before a small dragon steps out from behind the bushes on the top of the Rock of Ages where she has been hiding. Taking silently to the misty night air, she flies swiftly and low over the hills to follow the black car.

5:
METAMOR-
PHOSIS

In the large kitchen at No. 5 Maida Terrace, the hubbub increases as Lillian and Sebastian wake up to join in the conversation. After a while, the talk surrounding Willow's disappearance grows quiet as they eat, drink and listen to Jack recount the night's events.

'She's back, Magda Cross is back, who else could it be in the car?' he says.

'And it looks like she has captured another boy to train in her destructive and evil ways after we rescued the last one,' says Spellman.

'I was afraid this might happen. Wherever she is, foul beings will come or are already watching us,' Sebastian says quietly. 'It is good you are all here now and especially good to see you Branca.'

Branca smiles,

'And you too. Tell me more about Magda Cross.'

Meanwhile, Jack's twin sister Lottie lies asleep unaware of what is happening downstairs. Her dreams are a jumble of images full of people and places. Echoes of the last year of fighting against the evil ones come with random and disordered snapshots of scenes, still nightmarish and frightening. She tosses and turns, muttering in her sleep, then for a few seconds her vision is filled with Eda, King of the Wild Ones moving through a forest. It is accompanied by a feeling of great danger.

This small being and his people, have for centuries moved unnoticed through the rugged landscape of Andalucía, like shadows in the nighttime, shades in the sunlight. Making themselves known to Lottie and the others, they became allies during the adventures of last summer. A bond of deep friendship grew between Lottie and Eda and he showed her the Cave of Blank Windows deep in their underground caverns.

Lottie continues to twist about as briefly there is another vision, one she has had before of the Lady held captive who looks at her with such a beautiful smile. It brings her suddenly awake. Getting up and dressing with her mind still in turmoil, she struggles to clear it. Gradually becoming calmer then closing her eyes she feels an urgent need to concentrate hard to enter the dreamtime. An image of the lonely and wild place in the mountains of the Sierra Nevada near Eda's hideout slowly appears.

Suddenly she feels as though her mind is lifting her. Her body starts to feel as light as a leaf leaving a windblown tree, it's as though the very air around her trembles. Then comes a sensation of letting go, of flying, of great speed. A force pushes her. A force that can be heard and felt in the sounds of the wild, in the cry of the curlew, in the lonely howl of the wolf, in the tumble and roar of storming waters rushing. It is within all of those who can still listen, in jammed up cites as well as in deserts and forests, it is a pulse beating. After a short while it slows and comes to a stop.

There is silence and a calm stillness. A breeze touches her cheeks.

Lottie hears an owl calling.

Slowly opening her eyes, she looks up at tall trees looming darkly above her, the moon is high, the sky full of stars. Shocked by what has happened yet filled with an excitement that makes her want to shout, she nevertheless lies still and waits for several minutes. The forest is quiet.

Getting slowly to her feet, Lottie realises she is dressed in a warm cloak ready for the night chill. Looking around she finds herself in a glade surrounded by trees, with moon shadows slanting long across the ground.

There is a movement, almost imperceptible, then stepping out of a shadow Eda is there, as ever he is bristling with weapons. Walking just behind him on either side are his guardians, two enormous black boars with lethal looking tusks. About half her height he walks towards her, a big grin on his face to whisper,

'So, you are here. I was just thinking about you.'

'Of course, what did you expect?' She jokes smiling, her eyes radiant. 'What an experience, I actually managed to transmute to this place. I am not at all sure how I get back.'

Eda grows serious as he regards this tall girl with the friendly attractive face and wide penetrating eyes, her long fair hair still tousled from sleep,

'I think we might worry about that later although I am sure you will do it in a similar way. There is something here, close by in the mountains which is looking for us. I can feel its presence.'

'I felt it in my dreaming. How long has this been going on?' Lottie asks.

'Oh, only a few hours but it bears us no goodwill. I feel its hate.'

They begin to walk warily behind the two boars, who lead the way soundlessly through the dense forest until she hears the waterfall. Lottie picks up a frisson of anticipation as though everything in the wood is holding its breath. Very soon, they break through the trees into a clearing where the waterfall gushes over a cliff to disappear down the mountain.

Others are gathered there; Rezto, Eda's son and Rhaina his wife both rush up to greet Lottie. However, everyone's face is serious as they listen and wait. Eda is just about to say they should all move to shelter in the caves to let whatever it is pass by, when they hear a noise that mingles with the sound of the waterfall.

At first it is a low muttering as though several creatures are talking at the same time. Moments later a sinewy hand with long fingers that end in sharp claws, appears over the edge of the dark ravine into which the water flows. It grips the tall grass to pull itself up to reveal a long thin serpent's head, its forked tongue flicking out, its gleaming eyes fixed on them. Another arm appears to grasp at a bush, and then to their horror another head appears and then another and another until there are five of them. All the heads are on long necks that twist and turn separate ways at the same time before they all come to fix on the Wild Ones and Lottie. Then the hissing starts from every head, mouths wide, tongues flicking over sharp teeth.

'A Hydraphon; I didn't know they actually exist,' gasps Eda. 'Where did that come from?'

Lottie replies raising her voice above the noise,

"It must have been sent here.'

The rest of the creature is now fully out of the ravine, standing on its back legs, lit by the moonlight. The one who has been sent to find them is a fearsome and menacing sight, glistening with water droplets on its dark muscular body. Suddenly its tail lashes out to grasp a Wild One and squeeze. Immediately the others come alive and start to attack it, shooting arrows which only serve to annoy it further; the hissing increases as it moves forward.

'Lottie you must get away. Go now!' Shouts Eda, as drawing his sword he runs with the others towards the dreadful creature.

Lottie looks quickly around. She cannot get to the cave as the creature, without realising, is standing right in front of it blocking the way in behind the waterfall. She retreats, making her way back into the trees to watch, as the Wild Ones dodge in and out of the snapping heads trying to stab at the Hydraphon. The hail of arrows continues while others sneak out from behind the waterfall to join the fight. Lottie wishes the warrior Spellman was here.

Some of the Wild Ones are getting bitten, reeling away as blood gushes from their wounds. The one caught by the tail has been released as the others attacked but he lies still on the ground not moving. Lottie can see they will not win this fight.

Even though the black boars attempt to crash into it again and again, mostly they miss as it is agile enough to shift out of the way. They are both already covered in blood from the biting heads.

Then an even worse thing happens, Rhaina is caught up by the monster's tail. Although she is stabbing it as hard as she can it is having little effect. Lottie, the peaceful one feels the raging in her rise, it pumps through her as she watches. Trembling, her body shakes, her eyes shut and then it comes to her, the savage, the untamed and the brightly shining.

Eda is trying to reach Rhaina, she has managed to draw blood but her eyes are beginning to bulge. Several arrows have found their mark and two of the creature's eyes have been put out, although it has now started to move forward at a faster rate, stopping its hissing to concentrate on trying to kill the Wild Ones.

The Hydraphon is brought to a stop by a single roar; where Lottie was standing is a pristine Polar White Dragon. A dragon that is a little on the small side but is angry, very angry, seething with a passion to defend the Wild Ones.

They all scatter out of Lottie's way as she blows a white-hot fire at the five-headed monster. It drops Rhaina who rolls away as it tries to snap at the dragon, but the fiery white one takes off to hover and blast it again. One of the Hydraphon's heads erupts in a ball of fire as it attempts to jump up and bite the Dragon. Lottie hovers on top of it. The creature can only back slowly away as it tries to fight at the same time as dodging the fire. Eventually it is on the edge of the ravine. For a moment they both pause, the Hydraphon's remaining heads staring at the Dragon. Then the white-hot fire blows over it again making the monster step back, to fall over the ravine and silently disappear downwards into the dark.

Everyone hesitates, waiting, watching to see what will happen next as the waterfall continues to wash down the mountainside. The creature seems to be gone so others rush out of the cave to assist the injured. Eda leaps forward to help Rhaina, relieved to see her trying to get to her feet. The White Dragon looks around as though uncertain quite what she should do next.

Sometime later in the warm kitchen at No. 5, Branca is saying,

'Where is Lottie, I haven't met her yet?'

'Ah my sister can sleep through anything, but she will not want to miss this, particularly the news about Willow. It looks as though she and I were the last to see her as we said our goodbyes in the garden of the Spanish house last year.'

Lillian goes to see if Lottie is waking up but returns quickly to say she is not in her room.

'She will be on the roof,' Jack says. 'She often

watches the coming up of the sun, not that she will see much this misty morning. I'll go and find her.'

'Might I come too?' asks Branca.

'Of course, she will be very happy to meet you.'

Together they climb the stairs to the third floor which is in the roof. Entering Lottie's room Jack pushes up the skylight so they can clamber out into the mist swirling about the chimneys. As their eyes get used to the dark, they notice a figure sitting on a low parapet wall, a silhouette against the backdrop of the Suspension Bridge's misty light.

Lottie raises her hand and calls softly,

'I am here.'

Stepping carefully across to her, Jack introduces Branca and watches his sister's eyes light up for a moment, only to grow distant as though looking at somewhere beyond them. Knowing his twin sister's recent ability to enter the dreamtime he asks,

'What is it Lottie, what have you seen?'

She looks at them both directly with eyes that are still filled with surprise and awe. Saying with a slightly shaky voice,

'It's not only what I have seen, but where I have been and what I became.'

Jack looks puzzled but Branca asks quickly,

'Where is that Lottie?'

Jack watches his sister, seeing the light in her face as she explains what has happened to her and the fight with the Hydraphon. She finishes by saying,

'I felt incredibly happy, exhilarated, I felt the dragon was me and was what I am. It was my anger at the monster,' she pauses. 'A little scary perhaps coming on top of the force that took me there. I now understand what you felt like Jack finding the Great Grey Wolf was part of you.'

Jack, who is looking slightly envious of his sister, replies grumpily,

'I think your list of achievements far outweighs mine.'

Branca brushes that aside saying,

'It is unusual to achieve these things so soon. As you already know, many have achieved these levels of skill later in their lives, while others are planet bound evolving in different ways. Jack, I am sure your time will come to find and touch the force that will lift you.

'I will try to be a guide to both of you, help you to accept what your developing skills will bring. As a warrior I will also try to keep you safe. I am called the Shield Maiden; it is not an empty title. We will be invincible!'

They all grin at each other for a moment.

Jack is just coming to the end of telling Lottie about Willow when he suddenly becomes very still, his face etched with concentration. Holding up his hand he says,

'Can you hear it?'

Branca and Lottie look at him shaking their heads.

Jack with his high-pitched hearing, picks up a dragon cry like a vibration though the air.

'There is a dragon calling from somewhere nearby.'

Lottie is quick to say,

'Then it will be in the communal garden across the road.'

They hurry back down the stairs, past the kitchen and the murmur of voices, slipping out into the street to enter the tree circled garden through an iron gate.

Lottie points at a shadowy shape in a corner of the garden under an oak tree. As Jack walks towards it, out steps a small red dragon just slightly taller than him with a white blaze on its forehead, its eyes twinkling as he approaches. The twins first met this incredible creature with her dragon sister Synabeth and their father, the famous Ironjaw, last summer when their new life started.

'Gretchen,' Jack laughs softly, 'it is so good to see you.'

Branca needs no introduction as she is aware of Ironjaw's two daughters. The light is beginning to increase but the mist has become denser helping to hide the young dragon, so while Jack and Branca keep watch, Lottie talks to the winged messenger. Then silently Gretchen takes off, a dark shape in the foggy dawn.

Lottie returns to the others to explain,

'Ironjaw sent her today to help keep watch on what might be happening here. She arrived just in time to see you Jack watching the black car, so she followed it.'

Lottie quickly tells them of the meeting at the Rock of Ages, then says,

'After the meeting the car drove for several miles, before crossing a bridge over a wide reservoir and stopping at an isolated and grand looking house with a garden backing on to the lake. Gretchen has found a place to hide during the day so she will watch the house.'

'Was Willow there?' Jack asks as they move back into the house.

Lottie holds on to his arm,

'She didn't see her but perhaps she is, it was very dark,' she says seeing the anxious look on his face. Then looking at them both she adds, 'Can we just say the Wild Ones defeated the Hydraphon. For a while, I would like to get used to living with the White Dragon.'

6: A DANGEROUS GIFT

Inside the house everyone has moved to the large sitting room with its high ceiling, ornate fireplace, and the slow tick of a Grandfather clock. Lottie catches them up with Gretchen's information and Jack announces his sister's new skill and ability to transport herself.

They all look at Lottie, who blushes slightly before telling them about the attack by the Hydraphon. She finishes by saying,

'I also saw in the dreamtime a lady's face again for a moment. She was looking at me and smiling that wonderful smile, her arms were still held by strange claw like hands. I have now seen her several times, yet I have no idea who she is or what it means.'

Rodrigo asks Lottie to describe the lady's face a little more.

'Did she have a scar down one side of her face?' He asks.

'I don't know her hair was long and was partly covering her features.'

'Even so,' says Rodrigo looking at Sebastian, 'it does seem you may have seen your mother.'

A silence follows, broken by Sebastian who says,

'I hope it is Rhea. To stand any chance of rescuing her, we are going to need all our skills and resolve to defeat those that oppose us yet again.'

Rodrigo replies saying,

'I agree, but I would counsel we watch and wait a while for Gretchen to report before planning anything definite. Spellman and I have been called to a meeting with the leader in the council chamber. We should only be away a short time.'

In the garden across the road, by a bench seat near the communal barbeque there is lightness, almost indistinct against the light grey of the mist. It is a figure that glitters for a little watching No. 5, and then fades away with the mist as it begins to lift.

Meanwhile the house by the lake, hidden behind a backdrop of tall trees, is touched by early shafts of soft sunlight filtering through the mist. The Darkness comes skimming across the water towards it, undefined and massing like an immense cloud of starlings whirling in the early morning. It comes to meet its companion again, a beautiful elegant woman, as she stands waiting at the water's edge. Reducing itself, it swirls and dances around and envelops her, sighing its messages of affection and imaginings for the coming mayhem it wants to ensure.

Magda Cross's eyes burn red and glow, while her mouth opens wide, her long red tongue curling out as she utters a low menacing call that reverberates across the lake. At the edge of the mist, the water vibrates and erupts as a large dark green humanoid head breaks the surface followed by massive shoulders; it raises its webbed hand in salute and sinks back beneath the water.

'They will soon come,' she says, 'the fantastic ones on earth and water. They will bring fire and chaos. Look,' she points at the figure in the water, 'even that one comes.'

The Darkness spins away across the water, spreads out and comes back dancing and whirling, carrying images and sounds that are only for Magda Cross's eyes and ears. Cravenclaw and Smorkis raging and spitting fire, the fearsome Tigari centipedes moving through forests killing all, the Owlmen with their silent speed and deadly poisonous bite, the water creatures and those edging out of devil dreams, the nightmares of children. There are cities falling, the very earth burning and the wicked ones rising, all bound up together in a collage of evil. She sees them all.

The air moves and Magda Cross is her alter self, the chimera with two heads. One is a serpent and the other a rabid lioness emerging out of a strong scaly and winged body, with a long stinging tail. She stands on her hind legs, her serpent head blowing a brief gout of fire into the mist and out across the water. The Darkness flows over her in waves, hiding her. She revels in the images of destruction, and for a second or two something comes into the embrace of the Darkness. A vision of a huge shadowy figure appears, it points at her, it knows her, it knows her well, and it will consume all she is, promising her access and power beyond reasoning. In her mind she calls out,

'I am ready. Take the boy, take him, welcome him to the deep and hidden places of the night-time.'

The Darkness increases speed as it whirls around her, until she switches back to the tall elegant woman. The dark entity that has for so long yearned for substance and touch, envelops her in its shades and shadows. Then as fast as it came, it vanishes leaving her with a gift.

Magda Cross sighing deeply with a dark joy, turns to see standing behind her a Harlequin. He is tall with a diamond patterned costume of red, green and blue, a long dagger at his belt. He wears a black mask covering half his face, he looks like a jolly, if slightly scary pantomime character, but he is deadly. She has heard of him.

He bows low,

'I am your servant mistress.'

'Oh, you are very welcome here,' Magda Cross says.

'Thank you, I am sure it will all be a jolly jape.' He grins then says, 'You know you are watched?'

'Yes, and we shall give them something interesting to see very soon. As you say, it will be a merry dance, even if for them it will lead to their end.'

7: A COUNCIL OF WAR

The enormous planet Alpha revolves on its axis near the centre of the galaxy of Horizon. Its sea's ebb and flow, its land masses are green and verdant although some are scorched and hot. There are polar ice caps. Hold up a space mirror and you see a larger version of the planet Earth millions of light years away. It is a relatively comfortable world, a place where humankind and the higher animals live together, where myth is often reality.

In Menos, one of its ancient and beautiful capital cities, lays a magnificent hall with high and thick oak doors. It was built for the Council of the Wise, those who over centuries have grown to govern the Galaxy of Horizon.

It is the day after the meeting in the Bristol house. Adeth, a venerable man, a respected veteran of the war who is over two hundred years old, sits at the head of a table in the great council chamber. Even amongst these that live long, he is old, though his eyes shine with great intelligence.

As the leader of the council he surveys the group in front of him.

Darius, counsellor and universally famous hero of the wars with the Interventionists is sitting opposite him. He seems lost in thought. A big man, broad shouldered, he has a livid burn scar down the whole of one side of his face gained from fighting with the Ice Dragon. When he speaks, his words are trusted and revered as one who, at great personal cost, has a long experience of fighting for the Council.

It is said he lost his whole family to the black dragon Cravenclaw many years before. Ambrose found him wandering in a desert on some distant planet, talking incoherently about his wife and children. He rescued him, personally oversaw his rehabilitation, then mentored his rise through the Society of Protectors.

There are three others in the hall besides Adeth and Darius. Ironjaw the Red Dragon, Rodrigo, Morganast an exceptionally large spider who is there as a newly elected member of the Council, as well as Spellman. The warrior is also in attendance to give a report on the battle on Umorgo the Spider Planet. The report has been accepted and now there is a slight hiatus until Adeth asks Darius,

'What is on your mind brother?'

Darius shifts his weight in his seat, before replying slowly as though stringing random thoughts together,

'We are losing too much ground. What is left of our enemies is hidden on those lost planets that were once part of our Federation, just like Morganast's Umorgo which we have just been hearing about. The evil ones gather undisturbed in secret places to work against us. Many of the creatures created by the Interventionists to do their bidding, seem to be now controlled by others, or are free to roam where they wish.'

There is no dissent from anyone to this statement, so Darius continues,

'Although he was my mentor, my greatest supporter and I loved him dearly, I don't believe Ambrose or Rhea are still alive. Expecting them to return is likely to be an unfulfilled dream. Along with many others, I was not told where the twins were hidden until now. I think we should bring them out into the open to show how we have been protecting them since their parents disappeared. Every creature will then believe we are in earnest about fighting for the legacy of Ambrose.'

He stands up raising his voice, looking at each of them,

'We should stop being reactive. We should be attacking constantly as we did during the wars. Give me more Protectors. I will find the evil ones and drive them out into the open.'

Rodrigo replies quickly,

'I think it is too soon for Lottie and Jack to be exposed, they are not ready yet. It has been less than a year since they were made aware of their destiny and who their real parents are.'

The others nod their heads in agreement.

Adeth, stroking his white beard, slowly looks up at them all, his old eyes severe and serious when he says,

'I think Rodrigo is right, for the moment we need to keep the twin's whereabouts and exist-ence a secret from as many as we can. However, I also think Darius is right, that regardless of what has happened to Ambrose we should move on to increase the number of Protectors. Our brothers and sisters are hard pressed. They need help to fight those left behind who grow dangerous and desperate in the dark corners of the Universe. We must increase our vigilance, visiting those planets that were lost to us is now paramount.'

Morganast the great spider rolls his eyes and says in his cultured, precise voice,

'If there are other planets anywhere near the state Umorgo was in, then it is crucial to regain a foothold on what has been lost. Which Planets are you thinking we should visit?'

Darius looks directly at the tall spider whose several eyes watch him intently,

'Well, I think for a start the so-called Winter Planet would be one, then there is Langamar that is a wild and desperate place. Obviously, we need to keep the support up for your own planet Morganast, and even here on Alpha we are not in as much control as I would like to see. There are others of course dotted around the solar systems in our Galaxy, but we should start soon with these ones I have mentioned. Fortunately, although Horizon covers a massive area of space, the number of planets and moons is relatively small.'

'What about Hellviaka, surely given its huge size that must be on the list?' Rodrigo asks.

For a moment Darius pauses as though not quite sure how to react,

'I don't think we have enough strength in depth to go there yet,' he answers. 'It is extremely dangerous, a mysterious shrouded world right at the edge of the Galaxy where Beyond the Beyond starts. Where Space itself is empty, where there are no stars or planets. We will of course have to go there in the end.'

'Darius,' Adeth says, 'I would get the Councils support to increase surveillance and the numbers of Protectors. If necessary, we will fight to win back the lost planets and welcome them again into our Federation. It will need to be led by someone well known and a leader, therefore you should pick up that mantle to be responsible for its set up and completion.'

He looks at each of the others to see what they are thinking and all murmur acceptance of the plan.

Darius smiles and shrugs his shoulders,

'So be it, small groups are already searching when we have the time. I will start to recruit more now,' he says.

Spellman asks Darius,

'Perhaps Rodrigo and I might join a surveillance group for a short while to see how it works and maybe offer some advice?'

'Of course, you would be very welcome especially after your recent exploits. I know just the group for you to be involved with,' Darius replies smiling.

The red dragon Ironjaw speaks quietly,

'There is also the matter of the Darkness which we know has not been defeated. It still secretly gathers followers and seems to have endless power. Once they become part of its dark purpose, there is little chance of any of its disciples ever escaping. It kills any that try to get away from its malign hold over them.'

Adeth shifts himself to look directly at Ironjaw,

'I have not forgotten. I have heard from Rodrigo what happened yesterday with Lottie and am saddened to hear Willow is missing. We must defeat that dark shade, neutralising its influence which is becoming ever more widespread. A hard task as it just appears and then vanishes. I did wonder if it is quite as free as it would appear. I have heard others talking and speculating about it being controlled by another.'

Darius looks steadily at Adeth,

'That would have to be someone with great magic and power.'

Fingering his burnt face, he continues,

'I have also been given some information about the creature who gave me this; she has returned without success from the search for her children. My spies tell me the Ice Dragon now seeks out the Darkness to help find them.'

Adeth looks grim, but his old eyes hold the light of battle,

'Trouble comes ever closer so we must seek it out and destroy it. We must not let it grow and manipulate us into another pointless and savage war.'

8:

PAEDRENOSTRA

At the same time as the Council Meeting is taking place, on the Winter planet an immense Dragon has indeed returned, covered in ice she is spitting out fire and fury. Smorkis the Ice Dragon is magnificent as she rises on her back legs, screaming out from time to time in her agony, still raging at the loss of her progeny, calling out into the spinning and spiraling Galaxy.

'I will find out who you are! I am coming for you! You will not escape me.'

Utter silence greets this outpouring of anger although, after a while, ghost like creatures begin to gather to watch from a distance. They are upright, with pale oval faces having a cruel looking hooked beak while, through their empty eye sockets light gleams like a torch. These Shilocks are another humanoid copy created by the Interventionists to fight for them, and now left abandoned to their own devices. Their bodies are covered with a skin so tough the cold doesn't touch them; their strong arms end in claw like hands. They appear wraith-like as they cautiously approach the dragon through the ice and snow, making a collective humming noise intended to soothe the angry being.

As she calms down, the noise that Smorkis is making changes to a whistling, high-pitched communication, echoing out into the streams of space. The Shilocks gather in closer, happy to serve this raging creature. As they move in, there comes a turbulence of the air as though the very fabric and density of it is changing, and before them stands the fiercest black dragon of all, Cravenclaw.

Several days later, and thousands of light-years away on the lost planet of Langamar, the She-Dragon Paedrenostra uncurls herself to creep forward. Although she is unlike most other black dragons, she is the most feared of all the clan except for Cravenclaw. Her powerful, scaly thick bodied torso is like a huge long snake, carried on shorter legs while her tail is a whiplash. Flying fast she is quick and dangerous, an utter savage with a score to settle with one who is now walking straight towards her. The Protectors have come to Langamar seeking any black dragons or their allies. He is amongst them and coming within reach.

Paedrenostra's eyes gleam as she crouches right down, her mouth slightly open as though she is grinning, fire dribbles from it in anticipation. She waits, watching through the fire and rain as the steamy planet hisses and burns. The jets of earth fire, light the coming of the one she wants to kill, droplets of water running off his fighting suit.

Spellman and Rodrigo, after leaving the council meeting, immediately joined the group of Protectors on Langamar for a short time as suggested by Darius. On the last day of their mission they are searching for the enemy in an area that is inhospitable, cold yet fiery where storms are a constant feature. The two of them have found that the search by the Protectors for the followers of the Darkness is well organised. There are about twenty of them making camp for a day or two while they go scouting in pairs and reporting back.

Paedrenostra is not afraid of them. Knowing that he might be in the area is worth almost any risk. This is the human, who in the war came with his band and destroyed the She-Dragon's hold over 'her' villages. He with his soldiers liberated them from her rule, freeing them from feeding her frenzy for gold, and from supplying her constantly with food. Although she killed many Protectors, she was eventually driven away with Ironjaw's help, to hide in areas like this forbidding place.

However, the Darkness has whispered to her that her enemy can be found here, so she can seek her revenge. It was the Formless One who woke her from her centuries long sleep some thirty years ago. Binding her to him with his dark magic she joined the fighting against the Protectors.

Rodrigo and Spellman are taking a breather. Spellman has transmuted to be in full protector gear; the tough, flexible all-in-one armour suit like a second skin, the Dragon Sword is sheathed across his back, the Dragon ring on his finger. He is an imposing figure with his long dreadlocks, and he moves with an easy sway that speaks of power and agility. Rodrigo on the other hand, although a tall man in similar garb, also with a sword across his back, is somehow a less imposing figure. However, as with many he has a secret.

'I think we must be about three or four kilometres out from the camp and at the edge of our search area,' he says.

'This is the loneliest of places and it seems empty of anything dangerous to us,' says Spellman surveying the scene, as weak sunlight filters through the rain and steam. He grins, wiping the raindrops from his face, 'We have only today left to see any action before going back to Earth. I thought we might have spooked something out by now.'

'Mm, I think I'll settle for peace and tranquillity,' his partner grins back. 'Although I do agree with Adeth and Darius, it is obvious we need more of these surveillance groups to locate the disciples of death and destruction. One more sweep of the area should do it for us today, perhaps another thousand metres out and up into those black rock piles to the top of the hill.'

They split up, moving away but staying in sight of each other. Moving slowing they can see others in a long line doing similar, walking warily forward.

'A little closer,' she breathes, every muscle tense ready to leap on this man she has not seen for many years. Then, there he is, nearly on top of her so she launches herself with a roar of excitement into the air, a fire breathing, wing flapping, teeth snapping statement of power.

Spellman just happens to be looking towards Rodrigo and sees her leap forward,

'Look out!' He shouts starting to run.

Rodrigo looks up to see the great creature arrowing down on him. He manages to throw himself to one side and although the fire misses him, she hits him hard with her shoulder as she passes, knocking him flying, to roll over and over.

The Warrior is running fast drawing the Dragon Sword as he does so, others farther along the line are also moving towards Paedrenostra as fast as they can. She turns to come again at Rodrigo and is met by another roar this time from a great Grizzly Bear standing on his back legs, his mouth snarling, his teeth sharp and long, his eyes red with anger. For a moment she pauses never having seen Ro-

51

drigo like this before.

Then she is at him. The bear although large is nimble and dodges the fire stream to thump her hard as she passes, knocking her out of the air. She lands well, to rear up but before she can react the enormous bear pitches straight into her, and over they go, locked into each other biting and wrestling. The Dragons tail is thumping the ground and she is twisting trying to get a purchase.

The two adversaries suddenly spring apart neither getting a clear advantage on the other.

'Paedrenostra,' the Bear growls, 'I heard you were dead.'

'As you see it is not so,' comes the snarling reply. 'I live for days like these, and particularly to see you again.'

She breathes a gout of fire and fury at him, but he retreats ready for her to spring again. Which she does, flying straight into him, her talons digging into the Bear's shoulders, her mouth open ready to bite down hard. Rodrigo grabs around her body and squeezes hard with all his strength making her gasp for breath, then falling backwards still holding on to her. Crashing to the ground loosens his grip slightly, at once she squirms free, in a heartbeat she is in the air hovering ready to strike down. The great Grizzly Bear rolls away and stands up roaring ready for the fight to continue.

By now though, the others are arriving with

Spellman to form a half circle, swords drawn, bows pulled taught.

The Black Dragon does not understand the meaning of fear. However, she recognises the Dragon Sword and understands its power to slice easily through Dragon skin. She turns swiftly to climb through the black rocks until she is higher up and blows out more fire, snarling at Rodrigo.

'Never fear when all is done, I will come to claim you.'

The air moves, going out of focus and she is gone.

'She knew you brother,' Spellman says.

'Well perhaps not as I am now,' replies Rodrigo having returned to human shape. 'It is a story from a long time ago when I was fighting with Ambrose. I had heard she was dead.'

Spellman claps him on the shoulder saying,

'You must tell me some time, but I think we are done here for now.'

Rodrigo agrees, so together they gather their belongings from the camp, taking leave of their companions of the last two days.

That night as the moon is at its height, a large shadow raises itself from the ground to take down the two sentries on guard at the camp. Then it bursts in on the tented encampment breathing hell fire, biting and killing before any can transmute away. All are killed except one who is left to tell the tale of Paedrenostra's revenge.

9: NIGHTRIDER

Any insomniac denizens wandering the terraces and gardens of Clifton Village, would be intrigued and shocked to learn that during the night those shadowy movements, half seen at the edge of vision, are either wolf or dragon. The time while Rodrigo and Spellman were away has not passed idly for Jack, Lottie and Branca. Meeting together often, the Shield Maiden shows them techniques to let their minds travel also to protect against an invasion of their thoughts by such as the Darkness. Lottie has again found the way to transport herself and goes back to the house in Spain; even speaking to Miguel the gardener who appears not particularly surprised to see her. Jack remains frustrated by his inability to project himself beyond his environment.

In fact, they will remember this brief time as a pleasant lull before those hidden in the deepest dark seek to envelop them.

Rodrigo and Spellman return quickly to find little has changed on Earth. It is not until later they are made aware of the disaster that happened after they left Langamar. Rodrigo gathers the group to-gether to tell them of the fight with Paedrenostra and Darius's new role to actively seek out and destroy the evil ones. Finally, he says,

'Now, since the arrival of Magda Cross we have had a new terrifying creature, the Hydraphon seeking to wipe out the Wild Ones, then this dragon just happens to turn up at the same time as Spellman and I are on Langamar. She is an old enemy that I thought was long dead. I have been told that suddenly things have been going wrong with other patrols. It difficult to believe that it is just a coincidence.'

'So, you think someone or something, besides the Darkness and Magda Cross is orchestrating this?' Spellman asks.

'Yes, I think that is possible and they are trying to pick us off one at a time. We must be extra care-ful,' he shrugs. 'It is just a feeling which I find hard to shake off, that sometimes we are all being manipulated.'

'And you will have to watch yourself carefully Rodrigo, that She–Dragon will not give up I think,' Spellman replies.

Later to lighten their mood Sebastian who has become a football fanatic, although he has never kicked a ball in earnest, takes them to watch Bristol City play. A game they win with Jack and Lottie joining in the singing and chanting. Rodrigo is unimpressed, and Spellman asks why it's a penalty not a bonus point when an opposition player has been upended when he might score.

It is in this unlikely place that they are reminded of their mission and that they are watched. When they leave the ground with the supporters flowing out shouting and cheering, Jack spots someone he has seen before. Leaning with easy nonchalance, his hands in his pockets beneath the statue of the great England footballer John Atyeo, is a young man with a patch over his eye. He appears to be uninterested in them as though waiting for someone else.

As the others carry on, Jack draws Rodrigo to one side to point him out.

By the time they get back to the house the streetlights are on and it is dark. Recounting the sighting of the boy to Lillian and Branca who both elected to miss out on the football experience, the two women suggest it is time that some action is taken. Again, Rodrigo counsel's patience,

'Let them make the first move,' he says. 'For now, we must remain vigilant.'

In the morning there is nothing new from Gretchen. She has told Jack there is little movement at the house by the lake, except the car coming and going several times. Then comes another sighting of the wicked ones, this time at the University.

Sebastian is giving a lecture as one of the visiting Professors of Psychology and Neuroscience at the University. His talk that morning is one of several public lectures in the open day programme, allowing both members of the public and students in to listen. He argues and speculates about what the brain may be capable of, and how memory could receive help from being linked with artificial intelligence within a person. It engenders a lively debate about what might lie in the future.

He and Rodrigo have agreed to meet at twelve noon in the entrance to the University Tower that dominates the skyline, standing as it does on a hill above the city centre.

They meet just inside the grand wooden doors, as Great George booms out the hour and a large cohort of students descend the wide stone staircase. They are followed by a beautiful dark-haired woman whose arm is draped around a lad with a patch over his eye. Sebastian quickly pushes Rodrigo into a doorway. As she passes Magda Cross turns her head to smile sweetly at them, just for a second her eyes glow red. Then she and the youth are out of the doors and down the steps as a limousine pulls up for them to step inside.

'She teases us,' Sebastian says getting angry. 'Deliberately flaunting themselves so that we can see them.'

In the back of the car Magda Cross chuckles

wickedly and says,

'Who watches who? This game can go on and on, but Naptha the demon tells me she is ours now, our captive has come across so we will change the game.'

Harlequin, now looking like a rather handsome member of humankind, is driving the car and looks in the rear-view mirror to grin at her,

'They are confused and wait for us to make a move.'

'They will get their wish,' comes the reply.

At the beginning of that very night, as winter stars light the sky, a black cloaked rider is picking his way across the area of the Mendip Hills called Blackdown, an area of pine woods, bracken and farmland. His horse is thickset yet very tall, at least twenty hands high. Its eyes shine and glow in its massive head which is covered by an iron protective mask, by its side is the Black Mastiff. A seemingly lifeless creature wrapped in a thick pale cloak who has no interest in her surroundings, clings onto the rider. They seem to have come from out of the ground where the bracken is thickest and the shadow deepest.

Naptha the demon, his face like a skull, his eyes alight with a cold blue brilliance, spurs the horse into a gallop, he cannot resist calling out across the nighttime with a savage primal yell of triumph. He has wooed his prisoner with constant unremitting dreams and promises of power, and he believes he has emptied her memory of the lightness of being alive. She has been given another purpose. As they gather speed the black dog's tongue hangs out, flecks of spittle attaching to its fur as the air moves and shimmers around them and they are lost from sight.

Later the same night, the Great Grey Wolf is waiting in the cover of trees and scrub, watching across the Downs, all is still, dark and cold. By his side Gretchen looks at him sadly, as she gives him the news of the rider and the girl and a now empty house by the lake.

The Wolf wheels away as the dawn begins to break, ghosting his way back to Maida Terrace. There Jack enters to find an early morning conference in progress, with heated discussion going on again as to what should happen. They all look up as he walks in to tell them Gretchen's news.

Rodrigo asks quickly,

'And which way did the car go?'

'Evidently the car turned into Bristol Airport.'

There is quiet for a moment, in which the Grandfather clock's ticking fills the silence as the information is digested.

'Spain, I bet that is where they are headed,' says Lillian. 'They have had Willow under our noses all the time and now they want to move her.'

Lillian in her human form always appears as a friendly relaxed person, but she is shrewd, tough and relentless when faced with danger.

'Why?' asks Lottie.

'Good question,' Lillian responds. 'Perhaps they are choosing their battleground, expecting us to follow.'

'I think you are right Lillian,' Rodrigo says. 'I think we are meant to follow them. I can't believe they have let themselves be seen so easily without purpose. We are indeed being led to a battleground of their choosing, where they are more likely to be able to operate in secret.'

Spellman the warrior typically says,

'Then we should follow, wipe them out and rescue Willow. It must be her on the horse.'

They all grin; with Spellman things are often straightforward and simple to execute.

'As ever I respect your single-mindedness brother,' Rodrigo says laughing and then growing serious. 'I do indeed think we should follow but we will need all our resources. They have the advantage, and we need to restore everything to a more even level.'

'Of course,' Jack suddenly exclaims. 'They have to go by plane as well, the boy can't do otherwise yet.'

'And maybe never will,' adds Branca. 'He is not

from Horizon I think.'

'Who is the rider? asks Sebastian.

'I know who he is,' replies Branca a disgusted look on her face. 'He is Naptha, a demon, a horrible creature who can and will conjure up nightmares for Willow, spiced with the so-called dark joy of evil things. He will brainwash her. No one seems to know where he came from or how he got here. He is dangerous, a loner, loyal to no one, not even to the Darkness except if it benefits him.'

'I think we return to Spain tomorrow,' continues Rodrigo.' If you all go to the family house, Spellman and I will meet you later at the farm as we also need to warn Christine and Sergio.'

'Oh yes, it will be good to see those two again,' Jack says, 'although they will be disturbed to learn of Willow's disappearance.'

Christine has a small farm that lies within the great expanse of the Sierra Nevada Mountains. She is often seen with her long auburn hair tied behind her head as she walks her sheep to find grazing. She offers her horses for short treks across the hills and is helped by Sergio, a tough, tousle headed giant of a man. Although the farm is a lot higher up it is just across the valley from the twin's house. Sergio rescued Lottie from almost certain death, and Christine, captured by the evil Magda Cross was liberated by Willow and Lottie. Although both Christine and Sergio are earthbound humans, a deep friendship has formed between the five of them.

Rodrigo raises his voice to say,

'We have to find all three missing ones, Ambrose, Rhea and Willow.'

On the Winter planet, one of the lost planets in the outer reaches of Horizon where the Ice Dragon Smorkis comes to visit, two other creatures are also searching. They are looking across the freezing wasteland for a recluse, a hermit who might be able to help them. These Hobi rats are about a half metre in size with long inquisitive noses, bright bulbous eyes, sharp teeth and covered in white and black barred fur. Their names are Caramel and Hannibal, and they have a story to tell of the captivity of the woman with a most beautiful smile.

10: THROW OF
THE KNIFE

In Andalucía, the mountains and forests of the Sierra Nevada rise from the foothills of the Alpujarra in a wild landscape. In lower valleys, the rivers often run dry until the coming of the winter rain, yet the snow stays on the highest mountain tops in the hottest summer heat. The great ancient cities of Granada, Seville and Cordoba once flourished in this region as shining centres of the Earth's learning.

Perched high up in a tall tree, is a large fierce looking bird, a Bonelli's Eagle, her sharp eyes scan the rugged landscape pinpointing the slightest movement. Her name is Bonny, and she watches for the return of her great friend Rodrigo who found and rescued her after her parents were shot.

The Eagle is the perfect spy as she soars and glides on currents of warm air and then with incredible bird speed dives to fly low across the ground. She has seen the phantom rider on his great warhorse, riding with his passenger between the trees and out on the mountain. Bonny has also watched the huge shape that is Cravenclaw the Black Dragon returning to the area, shifting through the night sky when everything is quiet and sleeping.

When Rodrigo arrives at his simple mountain house with Spellman, Bonny is there. She lands on a rock and stretches to full height to look all around, before relaxing as the two men walk towards her. Spellman watches as Rodrigo and the bird look steadily at each other communicating through dreamtime talking. Bonny tells him about the secret journeys being made across the area.

Rodrigo looks up at Spellman to say,

'We should speak with Christine and Sergio pronto; they are in danger with these evil ones gathering. Bonny will keep on watching. Sebastian and the others arrive tonight, so I will call a meeting for us all at Christine's farm tomorrow.'

Later, Cravenclaw is also watching the now star lit landscape from his vantage point on the top of a mountain. His scaly long neck moves slowly from side to side until his fierce eyes catch sight of the approaching white SUV. Giving a satisfied grunt, he shifts his great muscular body to drift down the mountain towards the vehicle as it turns off the road, following a narrow track to a clearing in the trees by the side of a small river.

Magda Cross and Harlequin step out of the vehicle as the moon rises on this cold Andalusian night. The Black Dragon homes in over the trees to land close by.

'Mistress,' he breathes, his voice low and hissing, dark eyes sparkling with pleasure at the sight of Magda Cross.

'Hello, my faithful friend, as ever it is good to see you and we have much to do. I hear you have made a new friend.'

'I have found Smorkis the Ice Dragon. She will be with us. As we agreed I convinced her that the Protectors had caused her family to be destroyed, so now she hates them. Who is this with you?' The Dragon asks.

'My name is Harlequin. I have been brought here to help you win this fight and to capture the twins.'

Dressed normally in jeans, boots and jacket the humankind, although not fazed by Cravenclaw seems inconsequential compared to the great dragon who nods his head in welcome. He is more interested in Willow,

'What of the girl. Have we got her?'

Magda Cross smiles wickedly,

'We are nearly ready; she is ours now.'

Cravenclaw looks at her, his eyes sparking with anticipation of meeting the one who made a fool of him. It was Willow who sang the great creature to sleep, allowing Lottie to rescue Christine from the dragon's cave much to Cravenclaw's embarrassment and disgust.

There is a movement in the trees, and out of the dark shadows into the moonlight slowly walks the tall, muscular warhorse, followed at a short distance by the large mastiff dog. The horse comes to a halt in front of the SUV. The Demon Naptha turns to Willow,

'You may get down now my dear. We are among friends,' he says.

Harlequin steps forward to help her, supporting her to walk forward and stand shakily leaning against the car. Her eyes begin to focus, her face contorting a little, she smiles slyly at Magda Cross as though recognising a kindred spirit. As they put her in the back of the car Magda Cross says quietly,

'She is an empty vessel, but I will fill her mind with dark dreams and ambition; when she is no longer useful, we will discard her. I will make sure Spellman is there when we do that.'

She raises her arms to the sky as her eyes glow red with the thought of revenge on the Warrior. The Darkness streams across the Universe; it enters her head like a drug she craves, to bring her again a deep black joy.

There is a silence, only the river sounds, its waters burbling over rocks and stones to flow under an old fallen tree some distance away. In the deepest shadow below the base of the tree, an almost invisible small figure is watching. Eda, King of the Wild Ones waits and watches, just another shadow in the night.

Eda is too far away to hear them speaking. He remains absolutely still as the meeting unfolds; one of his guardians, a massive wild boar with huge tusks lies hidden nearby. Just as Eda is about to withdraw the scene in front of him changes.

Stepping into the moonlight is another awesome and horrific creature, a tall metallic humanoid which walks with a stooping, yet prowling purposeful gait. The front of its metal skull is shaped like a smaller version of the dinosaur Tyrannosaurus Rex, with rows of sharp teeth, although there is a curved extension at the back of its head which houses a large brain. Its body's entire trunk is metal, covering vital organs that are human. The creature's legs are bowed and jointed, ending with three toes with sharp metal claws, while its arms are long and powerful. A broad sword hangs from its belt and it carries a war axe. It is one of the most implacable of the Interventionists' creations; it hates itself and every human being. Behind it five other creatures that are smaller but equally fearsome stomp out of the dark woods.

'Welcome Dynasta leader of the Metalions. You and yours are a most welcome sight,' Magda Cross oozes charm.

"What is that human doing here?' The metal one spits out furiously, its eyes suddenly blazing with anger.

Before any answer is forthcoming, one of the Metalions lopes across towards the Harlequin, now in his pantomime red and black diamond apparel. Picking up speed as it goes and raising its axe, the creature has only one thing on its mind, to kill the human being. The Harlequin grins at it and in a blur, spins round and suddenly a knife is flying through the air. It embeds itself with deadly accuracy in the eye of the onrushing Metalion, who falls stone dead without making a sound.

Magda Cross erupts, shapeshifting to her chimera being. Rising on her hind legs she rages at them all, her reptile head spitting fire and her lioness head glaring at them,

'You will not fight amongst yourselves,' she hisses. 'You are ordered by the Master to be here and only he decides who lives, who dies.'

For a moment, as if from nowhere, a fierce wind batters them and is gone.

Dynasta growls,

'So be it, I hear you. We won't miss that one.' He points at the dead Metalion, 'there are many more of us that can come here.'

The watcher under the tree silently backs away

and with his guardian melts into the night.

At the Boulter farmhouse, there is much activity unpacking their old Land Rover after the ride up from Malaga; it is midnight and wood is being brought in and fires lit to warm the cold house. After eating a quickly prepared supper, Jack and Lottie walk outside to show Branca where they first encountered Gretchen's sister Synabeth and where it all started. Dressed in warm jackets, they all three look out from the end of the swimming pool, on the clear starry night at the mountains whose tops are covered in deep snow.

'Beautiful,' breathes Branca, 'but out there somewhere are our enemies and our friend.'

They gaze up at the vast landscape.

'Tomorrow we start our search for Willow,' Jack says. 'We will all meet at Christine's.'

The next afternoon the weather has changed, and pouring, chilly rain is splashing off a beaten-up red van and the old Land Rover Defender as they battle their way along the mountain track to Christine's farm. Pulling up in the yard, the door of the house is wrenched open, and standing there is a giant of a man with a big grin on his face, followed by a young woman with a mass of auburn hair.

Sergio and Christine usher the visitors inside to a large room with a log fire burning brightly. In the excitement Christine's welsh accent becomes ever more pronounced as they all crowd in, back slapping and hugging each other. Branca is introduced to them both. She grins as she recognises the warmth and affection that they all have for one another, battle hardened by the previous summer's exploits.

Christine has coffee and food at the ready, so they all find somewhere to sit with their steaming plates of hot goulash. Between delicious mouthfuls, she and Sergio are caught up with the events of the last few weeks and the shock of Willow's disappearance.

Sergio says, speaking English with a Spanish lilt to it,

'Things here have been quiet. Eda will occasionally turn up, appearing from nowhere it seems but we have not seen Agnes since you left. No dragons, no Magda Cross and no devil centipedes thank goodness!'

'All that is about to change Brother,' Spellman the Warrior says, his eyes glittering.

'At least it won't be such a surprise this time,' Christine replies. 'But tell us what happened after you left us. Did you manage to keep your promise to go back to the planet where you found the Dragon Sword and met the giant spiders?'

Several others murmur and nod their heads at that request.

Spellman surveys the group and says,

'Yes, I did go back to help them fight the red plague and Branca came with me. Ironjaw, his daughters and other Protectors had already gone before us. You will remember that in the fight with the Water Scorpion for the Dragon Sword I was forced to leave my good friend, the spider Shaila. She was desperately wounded, but she begged me to go taking the sword with me.'

He looks around at them all as they settle to hear the story.

11: SPELLMAN, BRANCA AND THE SPIDERS

Two months previously Spellman and Branca, upon arrival on Umorgo found themselves involved in a fight. They had arrived in a clearing in the jungle, where in front of them two giant spiders were fighting a large group of enormous, poisonous red ants in complete silence. Surveying the scene, Spellman says,

'The spiders are unaffected by the ant poison but their bite is still vicious.'

'Look at that,' Branca points, 'they are attempting to get on the spiders back to bring them down, stopping them from spinning their webs and biting them.'

'Here we go!' Shouts Spellman as they start to run forward drawing their swords dodging those giant ants that are already enshrouded in webs.

The two Protectors pitch in, fighting their way

towards the spiders, whirling and swiping, twisting and turning, keeping well out of the way of the ants' poisonous bite. They wreak desperate damage on the red creatures, killing nearly all of them very quickly. The last two run fast across the ground making for the cover of the jungle. One of the spiders bending her legs, takes off leaping through the air to land on top of them both, pinning them to the ground and ripping off their heads with her beak-like mouth.

Branca looks at Spellman grinning,

'Now that's what you call a jump.'

The remaining spider speaks in a very cultured soft voice to say,

'Thank you, my friend, but you are a bit late the war with these creatures is almost done, especially after the coming of Ironjaw and his daughters. Not that we don't appreciate you being here.'

This was followed by a low husky chortle that a stunned Spellman instantly recognised.

'Shaila is it really you? I didn't think I would see you ever again,' he said, staring at the great creature's front legs.

'Ah, the legs. It is simple biology; when we are young our limbs grow back,' although as an afterthought she murmured, 'these are still quite stiff.'

'But you were at the mercy of the Water Scorpion how did you survive?'

'Now there's a story,' the returning spider says.

'Leptis,' Spellman shouts. 'It's good to see you again too. But wait, let me introduce you to Branca she has come to help in the fight.'

The two spiders' six eyes sparkle,

'You are very welcome. We have just seen that you might be useful in a fight,' Leptis chortled. She continues to say, 'As you left, and I was trying to draw the Scorpion away from Shaila, I caught sight of this strange white light which appeared on the veranda of the old house at the end of the lagoon. The next thing I knew, a silver arrow is flying which strikes the Scorpion. The creature roared in pain for a moment, then just turned around going back to the lagoon to sink beneath the waves.'

'I saw that light too very briefly as I was leaving you both,' said Spellman.

'Perhaps the winged ones who used to live here are returning,' said Shaila. 'But now we need to turn to the business in hand. The war goes well. Ironjaw and my father Morganast are leading the battle against the red scourge that are now fighting a rear-guard action. We know they have sent a group ahead of them to secure the mountain at the top of the lagoon. It is an extremely hard place to attack.

'We think the ants are protecting one of their queens as well. If they get there, they can establish a base, start to breed again and regain their strength. So, we were on a scouting mission to see how far they have got when we were set upon by these ones.' She points a foot at the dead ants.

'It is obvious we do not have the time to report back. They are further on than we thought,' Leptis says.

'Then we head them off,' Branca says. 'We stop them.'

'Yes,' agrees Spellman.

As he speaks two more spiders appear at the edge of the jungle, Dreadfoot and Sperry, two males who have turned up in response to an earlier call for help from Leptis.

Spellman grins,

'Four Spiders, two humans; a match for anyone.'

The six of them led by Shaila move quickly and cautiously along paths and trails heading towards the Lagoon. The hot and humid jungle is unusually quiet, broken only by occasional screeches of some exotic bird. Quite soon Spellman sees the waters of the Lagoon glittering through the trees, and moments later they arrive at the edge of the vegetation. Coming to a stop they look out across a hundred and fifty metres onto the passive stretch of water, a gentle breeze rippling its surface.

'There's the house where we found the old boat that I used to get to the Island to find the Dragon

Sword,' Spellman says to Branca, pointing towards the southern shore of the water.

'And there is the mountainous land the ants will head for as they are driven out of the jungle.' Shaila points to the northern shore where they can see a small mountain set in a rugged landscape. 'There are many places, caves and valleys beyond that mountain they can hide in to grow strong again and for the Queen to lay her eggs. I hope we are not too late.'

'Indeed, we are not. Look there.'

Branca points down the shore towards the southern end. Pouring out of the jungle is a large group of red ants with some of their leaders over two metres plus in length. The Interventionists had changed the ants' genetic code to grow these creatures to become their servants and soldiers. Now they are left to their own devices.

'I see no queen ant with them,' says Shaila. 'Maybe she has already grown her wings and is now up on the mountain laying her eggs somewhere. However, we can't worry about that now, we need to finish these ones off.'

The vicious red creatures are moving swiftly, spread out between the vegetation and the water, increasing their speed now that they have caught sight of the mountain. There is about thirty or forty of them who come to a sudden halt, rising on their back legs to see the way, an awesome sight.

The Shield Maiden does not hesitate, in full protector gear she is running fast straight at them. Shield on her arm, sword raised as she pounds down the beach flanked on each side by a giant spider just about keeping pace with her. Branca is in amongst the insects like a whirling dervish, turning and twisting, slicing and stabbing. The two spiders Leptis and Sperry hit moments later stamping and biting.

As the surprised giant ants reel backwards and try to organise themselves into groups, they are hit from behind as Spellman, Shaila and Dreadfoot join the fight. The red ones are soon falling, caught in a bloody sandwich by the furious onslaught.

Spellman looking up notices one of the leaders escaping, moving fast along the shore towards the mountain. Leaving the fight, he gives chase pursuing the ant along the water's edge. Then he hears it, a loud whirring noise behind him. Turning around to look up he sees the Queen, mighty in flight, three metres long flying out of the jungle. She is furious, flying straight towards the Warrior ready to drop on him. An incredible and fearsome sight, she hovers over him, he can see her mandibles opening wide.

Backing away sword raised, the warrior trips and falls sprawling on the beach, the Dragon Sword is shaken from his grip to land some distance away. The escaping ant turns to come back and join its Queen. Spellman is just thinking things couldn't get any worse when the water erupts, and out comes his old enemy the dreaded Water Scorpion the previous guardian of the Sword.

Branca is running towards Spellman watching this huge creature with its massive serrated pincers as it rises out of the water to stand over him. She knows it is a futile gesture, she won't get to him in time to help. Then it happens; the Queen caught completely by surprise, is knocked out of the air by one of the Scorpion's callipers. The great creature is on her in a trice, she has very little chance as it's stinging tail stabs down. Branca doesn't stop and manages to catch and dispatch the leader that had escaped. She turns around to see Spellman carefully rising to his feet.

He is facing the Water Scorpion whose large bulbous eyes never waver from watching him. The sword is lying at least three metres away. Branca can see he is trying to edge towards the weapon. She starts to shout to distract the Scorpion as the Spiders come up to join them.

As they move towards Spellman a strange thing happens. The creature ignoring everything else picks up the Dragon Sword gently in its pincer, looking lovingly at it then at Spellman. The Warrior is completely taken aback as it holds out the Dragon Sword towards him. He hesitates but then it pushes the sword at him again. Reaching out to take it Spellman is expecting the other pincer to take his head off, but nothing happens. The Water Scorpion allows him to take it back. They look at each other for a moment and then the great creature turns slowly, makes its way down the shore to sink back into the water and is gone.

Branca reaches him quickly. He is still standing with a puzzled look on his face staring at the surface of the water.

"Why?' He manages to say.

'Because it knows you are now the guardian of the sword it adores. It has passed on to you and you wear the ring,' says Shaila.

12: FOUND
YET LOST?

'After the fight with the red plague there was an amount of mopping up to do,' Spellman is saying. 'We met up with Ironjaw and Morganast to help finish the job, then headed back here, leaving with all sorts of plans being made to bring the lost planet back to something like its former self.'

There is a brief round of applause from the listeners as the rain continues to beat at the darkened windows. Christine stands up, her long auburn hair shinning in the fire and candlelight to say,

'You will all have to stay the night as the roads will be nearly impassable for a while. We can make you very warm and comfortable in the barn again.'

There is a general nodding of heads at that, when Branca says,

'Christine, I have a present for you.'

Taking Christine by surprise she reaches for her long bag and pulls out a beautiful sword that glints in the firelight and hands it across.

'We know you have elected not to have your memory of us wiped. Also, you can't transmute and there is always danger, so we thought you should have this. I will teach you how to use it. It is a present from Rodrigo, Spellman and me.'

Nothing is said, the two women face each other and clasp hands, and the deal is done. Sergio looks on proud of his best friend, almost a sister.

The rain beats at the windows but Jack hears a feint scratching.

'Shush!' he says, and as all goes quiet he raises a lantern to the window, and there looking back at him is a forlorn and twisted face with sodden hair.

'Willow!' he shouts.

Spellman is first through the door to return carrying a soaking wet and shivering Willow. He puts her down in a chair by the fire, she is hardly conscious and is mumbling about a creature called Naptha and being very cold. Christine and Lottie take her into the spare bedroom to dry her off and put her into bed. They try to give her some hot goulash, but she will only take water and soon falls into a sound sleep.

The group is quiet, not sure what to make of this turn of events.

Branca says,

'We know about Naptha the demon of course.

She has obviously been his prisoner for some time; I wouldn't envy her that. She needs to sleep now. But how did she get back here and was she followed?'

'Where is Jack?' Lillian suddenly asks.

They hear a wolf howl, already a long way off.

The Great Grey Wolf is a large shadow gliding through the woodland with the rain still pouring down, there is no wind, the black night is bleak and absolute. Following the track hidden in the trees, nothing moves bar the Wolf, ears cocked for the slightest noise above the falling rain. Jack had also wondered how Willow had got there and if she was followed. Suddenly he hears a horse's hooves coming slowly around the bend and he smells a dog.

Going to ground, he watches the huge horse and the dark cloaked rider come into view and stop, the black dog catching up to them to stand sniffing the air. Naptha the Demon, with the rain running off his hooded head looks steadily around, his bright piercing blue eyes taking in the silent dark trees. The dog's low growl rumbles across the night.

'I know you are here somewhere,' the Demon says, his voice echoing through the wood. 'Tell my new disciple that I will come for her, she will not be with you long. She cannot escape from me or from what is coming. You should give her back to me, she will be safer in my care.'

The Wolf stays completely still the hair on the back of his neck rising in anger. Other grey shapes have answered his earlier call, moving slowly towards him and his enemy, so that soon there is a wolf pack almost surrounding the rider. Naptha simply laughs, rears his horse up, wheels it around shouting this time,

'Tell her I will see her soon!'

The horse's hooves drum the ground as it gallops away with the black dog keeping up with the pace. The Great Grey Wolf watches as they disappear around the bend and then turns to lope back through the trees to the farmhouse, his companions following, drifting through the night as the rain begins to ease off.

It is late when Jack enters the house to find Lillian sitting by the fire waiting for him. He immediately feels a frisson of danger.

'Where have you been Jack?' Lillian asks. 'You look worried.'

Jack tells her of his encounter with Naptha and then says,

'There is something wrong here, I felt it as soon as I walked back in. We are in danger. Willow has brought something in with her.'

Lillian also has misgivings herself about Willow just turning up but says,

'We will have to wait until the morning. The others are sleeping in the barn where there is plenty of straw and blankets, you should get some rest.'

Jack replies,

'I am not tired. I will stay around outside with my brothers and sisters for a while.'

'Then I will sleep here,' Lillian says.

She opens the door to check on Willow who is tossing and turning despite being sound asleep. Lillian stays in the room for a little while watching, when suddenly Willow's eyes open to stare at the ceiling. Unaware of Lillian's presence, she whimpers as her eyes widen for a moment, and her hand raises as though trying to protect herself against something she does not want to see. Her eyes close again but the tossing and turning continues. Lillian strokes her hair and her forehead until she seems to rest, her breathing becomes softer, she mumbles some indistinct words in a whisper, which sound like,

'I am Willow, the singer of songs that lull dragons to sleep……'

It tails off and eventually she sighs and falls into a deeper sleep.

Outside the rain has stopped and the night is becoming clear as the clouds roll away. The Wolf lies down near the back wall of the house, other eyes gleam in the dark at the edge of the wood as some of the wolf pack join him. Suddenly he is aware that someone else is moving quietly out of the barn to come and sit on a bench near him. Branca dressed in warm clothes against the chilly night air nods to him, and they sit in companionable silence and watch the night for signs and portents of danger. Much later in the distance, as the first streaks of dawn come into the sky, a dragon briefly roars out its challenge and then falls silent. The Wolf and the Shield Maiden do nothing but wait and watch.

A light shape, almost, but not quite a figure comes into the trees, it moves over the ground, shyly it comes close to them sending signals that spark deep in the eyes of the Wolf. Branca sits up and holds her hands out as though warming them in front of a fire. The light shimmers and grows larger for a second or two then gently fades. The two watchers feel their heart beats quicken, not sure what they have seen, but energy and warmth pulse through them both. The wolves around the wood stand up to look at the Great Grey One who moves and nods his head to one side, so they begin to lope back into the landscape.

Both Branca and Jack, who has now changed back, overawed by what they have just seen quietly enter the farmhouse. Lillian and Christine are making coffee and the log fire has been rekindled. The others appear and Jack tells them about the visit of the Demon Naptha. At the mention of his name the door to the bedroom opens and Willow stands leaning on the doorpost saying,

'I fought him you know. I fought him so hard and I managed to keep a piece of me he couldn't touch.'

Christine grabs her before she falls and puts her in a chair by the fire. She hands her a warm drink saying,

'Take your time it can't have been easy.'

Willow sighs and shudders,

'You have no idea the endless painful searching in my head. He tried to own me with his promises of power and success, trying to break down my reason. There was so much noise in my head at times I just wanted it to go away. He told me I was abandoned by you all and you would not welcome me back. Then the ceaseless noise would come again.'

Lottie says,

'Oh Willow, we are so glad and relieved to have you back but how did you get here?'

Looking at Lottie for a moment her eyes well with tears and there is just a hint of fear.

'I have seen such things,' she says, then shakily and hesitantly tells them what happened when she met Magda Cross.

They all listen carefully until she finishes with,

'While the chimera was raging, I was pretending to be asleep so they were ignoring me. I just opened the rear door of the car in all the noise and slid out. They didn't know I could still transform, so as a mouse I ran into the undergrowth and disappeared. I ran and ran for all I was worth and found my way here. I saw that creature Naptha searching for me with his black dog which almost found me until I hid in a hole.'

Spellman comes to sit close by, holding her hand as she shakes and shivers although the room was warm.

'I think enough for now little one you need to rest, we need to get you well,' he says looking closely at her.

Spellman and Willow have a special bond since she welcomed him as a self-imposed guardian and mentor after she joined the Protector training school. Her parents also Protectors disappeared, probably killed during the war, leaving her to be brought up as a four-year-old orphan. She rose to be a star pupil at the School where the Warrior recognised her skills and bravery.

He helps her up and Christine guides her back to the bedroom; at the door she turns, her eyes narrow as she says,

'They knew you were watching them. They know where you are.'

Then looking directly at Jack her voice begins to rise becoming almost hysterical,

'Why did you not find me? Why did you not look for me?

Christine puts her arm around her shoulders and eases her into the bedroom as Jack tries to say,

'I didn't know you were missing. I would have ....'

Then he is stopped as Christine shakes her head and Willow collapses against her.

Lottie looks across at Jack's anguished face and a signal passes between them.

The others begin to discuss what they have heard while Lottie says,

'I need some of that mountain air.'

Opening the door and stepping outside, she enters a different world where the sky is now a cobalt blue and the sun is hitting the mountains with rays that rebound off the snow that has fallen on the peaks. The air is clear and cold.

A little later as the group continue to talk, Jack's superior hearing brings him the high piping sound of Lottie's silver whistle given to her last summer by Eda. She is calling him and others of his clan to come. Jack looks around, no one else has heard it. Still shocked by Willow's outburst, he moves across to the chair by the fire gazing into the flames and embers looking for a sign. He smiles grimly to himself acknowledging he does not have his sister's skills and promptly falls into an exhausted and disturbed sleep.

13: SILENTLY FALLING

An eagle lands in a tree making Lottie look up and raise her hand to greet Bonny. Then they come, two huge Black Boars step out of the woodland, followed by two of the Wild Ones armed with knives, a sword and a bow with a quiver of arrows. They are dressed in greens and browns with calf length boots. Eda, King of the Wild Ones and Rezto his son, greet Lottie as they sit down at an outside table. As Sergio comes out of the house to tend to the horses and sheep, Lottie motions for him to sit with them.

'We need your help Eda,' Lottie says, but before she can continue, he says,

'We were on our way here to warn you when you called. What is being released here is malevolent, dangerous and menaces us all.'

He tells them of the meeting he spied on between Magda Cross, Cravenclaw and the Metalions after the Demon turned up with Willow, unwittingly corroborating what Willow had already told them.

'I didn't hear anything they were saying though, I was just too far away, except when Magda Cross obviously threatened them all after one of the Metalions was killed. One minute the Metalion was running at a strangely dressed human, the next it is lying dead. Some sort of altercation I guess; it would seem all is not well in the camp of the unlovely.'

'Did you see Willow's escape out of the back of the car where she says she was put after being taken off the horse?' asked Lottie.

'She's escaped,' Rezto exclaims, 'that is good news!'

'Indeed,' said Eda, 'but I think I was gone by then. She was certainly in the back of the car. I did hear Cravenclaw's roar this morning, but I think that was just to tell you he is here. You are supposed to be afraid.'

Sergio gets up from the table saying,

'I will finish doing the animals then join you inside, I think we need to move quickly.'

He moves off towards the stables as Lottie nods her agreement.

Lottie is suddenly dreaming, staring into the distance concentrating, as the noise of the mountains, the bird calls, the rustling breezes and animal noises recede. In her mind an echo of someone crying reaches her. A feeling of terrible sadness sweeps over her as she realises the tears are her own. Next, there is a vision of a wood where she is desperately trying to look out through the trees. The images are blurred making it impossible to see what is happening. Lottie tries to run forward to reach whatever it is that lies beyond. Struggling to move her feet that feel like they are glued to the ground, then calling out she finds her voice is a whisper. The vision changes momentarily, Iron-jaw the great Red Dragon is there blowing fire. For a few seconds she feels his strength before the picture fades, and she is back with the two Wild Ones. They are looking at her as Jack comes out to join them.

Shaking slightly, she tells them what she has felt and seen. Eda, his bearded face looking at her seriously, holds her arm before saying,

'It's hard to decipher what it might mean just now, perhaps it will become apparent later. We must go to warn our people and get them ready. Lottie, you know how to summon us and of some of the places we are found.'

With that the two Wild Ones take their leave walking into the trees with the guardians.

Jack says,

'When I went back in this morning, I still felt the danger.'

Lottie looks at him and hugs him,

'I don't know what it is Jack, but it seems we are being manipulated somehow and it is very scary.'

Jack looks at her,

'But Willow is so changed and the possibility of her being a danger, well, I just can't believe it.'

He looks a little lost.

Lottie replies,

'I know what you think of her Jack. What we all must realise is that she has been through an awful lot which we can't begin to imagine. It may just be an aura that she carries with her, left over from her time with the demon. We will get her better and strong again, then we'll see.'

Jack shrugs and smiles at his sister.

Back in the house Lottie tells them that she thinks Ironjaw is on the way, Rodrigo looks at her closely saying,

'I think that too and with his daughters. I know where they will be and will go to meet them to tell them what is happening. I will also see if the old ruined fort we used before is still uninhabited and reachable. Spellman it would be good if you came too.'

Spellman hesitates, Lillian seeing his reluctance says,

'I think we should take Willow away from here

and establish a base again at our place across the valley. She is very disturbed and needs rest to recover.'

'I think it is a good idea to get her away,' Rodrigo agrees. 'If you leave quickly in the Land Rover you should be safe enough. It is unlikely any of these evil creatures will be about on the main roads in broad daylight. I think the rest of you can stay here, by tonight we will have more help with the coming of the dragons and then we can defend ourselves in two places if necessary.'

Spellman, torn between staying with Willow and going, agrees.

Sebastian claps him on the shoulder saying,

'Don't worry, I know we are not fighters but we have a bite.'

Spellman grins, the two Protectors alter beings are the same, and a mongoose is extremely fast with a nasty bite.

Branca says quietly to Christine,

'It won't be a wasted day. I'll start to teach you some moves with the sword.'

Everyone begins to move about their tasks. Christine goes into the bedroom to wake Willow, who she finds is already dressed in a change of clothes that were left for her. Outside the Boulter family are hugging each other with exhortations to be careful and stay safe. Willow is installed in the back of the Land Rover, Sebastian fires it up and they are off. Jack and Lottie watch them go as a last wave comes out of the window from Lillian.

In another part of the mountain Dynasta the Metalion prowls purposefully through the woods with his semi crouching but powerful gait. His watchful, greedy eyes are gleaming. Woodland creatures hide from his coming. He makes little noise except his breathing is heavy and laboured, but the Darkness is in him spurring him on.

Back at Christine's, Rodrigo is with Bonny the eagle who is perched on the lowest branch of the tree. Soon the bird takes to the sky, rising high into the blue until she is a black dot. Spellman and Rodrigo leave about thirty minutes later to head up into the mountain in the old red van.

Meanwhile Lillian and Sebastian are joining the morning traffic going down the mountain. They reminisce about how it was when they first came to earth, trying to engage Willow in conversation. However, she just gives monosyllabic answers as she watches the countryside pass by. Eventually the one-sided conversation peters out and there is just the noise of the engine in the cab, until suddenly Willow yells out,

'There, in there, that's where we met with Magda Cross and the others. Let's look and see if there is anything left that we could use to find them.' She is pointing at a wide track.

Sebastian slows the Land Rover and looks at Lillian who shrugs saying,

'It is as the man said broad daylight.'

They turn the Land Rover around to go back and get off the road. The vehicle chugs slowly along the track for a short distance, rounding a bend into an empty grassy clearing above a cliff edge which drops sheer to the valley below. It is screened from the road by thick trees. Lillian and Sebastian have no idea that it is not the same place at all.

They drive into the middle of the clearing and stop, looking out of the windscreen over the view from the precipice. The day is bright and clear, they can see for miles. As they look outwards towards the shining horizon something slams into the back of their vehicle. The back of it begins to lift and be pushed slowly forward towards the edge of the cliff. The three of them reel around and see the worst thing possible, the huge bulk of Dynasta, his mouth wide open showing rows of huge teeth. He is breathing heavily from the exertion of trying to push them all over the edge.

Lillian and Sebastian have the briefest of seconds to look at each other as they clasp hands tightly, he kisses her forehead. Then they are out of the doors shouting at Willow to run for it, as they change and two large mongooses run at the Metalion.

They attack him from both sides, trying to run up his metal body to reach his face, forcing him to stop pushing the truck to fend them off. Then another Metalion lumbers out of the trees and grabs them both by the scruff off the neck. They scrabble to hang on to Dynasta still trying to bite into his face prolonging the time Willow has to escape. The Metalion holding on to them is too strong and wrenches them away from its leader flinging them into the air and out over the precipice. Only one small squeak is heard as they fall silently over and over towards the valley floor. Bonny arrives just in time to see them falling and she swoops down towards them.

Willow runs as fast as she can along the track as Dynasta and his companion push the Land Rover over the cliff edge, to fall bouncing and crashing off the mountain, until the trees slow it and it comes to a stop on its side. Dynasta growls loudly and raises himself up lifting his arms to celebrate his triumph.

A white SUV approaches the entrance to the track and pulls over just as Willow makes it to the road. A beautiful woman's face leans out of the back window,

'Well done daughter, all has worked perfectly,' Magda Cross says. 'Now, find your way back to the others.'

Willow gives her a sly smile, her face contorted,

her eyes rolling back in her head showing the whites of her eyes. She begins to walk along the mountain road until she disappears back into the trees.

Bonny has come to rest sitting on the lowest branch of an oak tree. She hears Dynasta's growl and looking up at the cliff sees his arms raised to his Master, as the Darkness swirls around the metal creature. The bird's head swivels downwards to look at the broken bodies returned to human form. Sebastian and Lillian are lying quite close to each other near a stream that continues to gurgle on by. The sun shines and a gentle breeze plays with Lillian's hair, her eyes gaze sightlessly at the sky.

14: THE HERMIT AND THE WIND HORSES

While a disaster plays out on Earth, on the Winter Planet the two Hobi Rats Hannibal and Caramel are watching the early evening sky with its radiant aurora of changing colours, as the moon and its two satellites rise. The luminous colours reflect on their fur as they look out onto the frozen waste. The fierce winter storms are grown quiet for a while on this lost planet so far from its sun, which only manages two months of summer.

These two are waiting for a message, the word will come. There are hundreds of Hobis spread in warrens across the landscapes of snow, hidden and camouflaged in their black and white fur, lost to sight in the weak light of the sun and shade.

Hannibal and Caramel have heard about the mysterious human called the Hermit. They feel sure that if they can find him, he will be able to help the woman captive. Their whispered message for information gets passed along the line, spreading out over the community. Eventually, a tired and exhausted Hobi called Lennie arrives after sunset with news of where they might find him.

'He lives perhaps two days away from here in the land of the hot springs and the warm lake Mirramor. He seems to be always on the move, so he is difficult to find as he is never in one area for long. However, it seems the hermit does have some special places that he frequents more than others. We, who live nearby do not fear him but he is distant and difficult to approach. He is by himself.'

Hannibal says,

'Come in friend Lennie, rest and eat, we will speak some more about this person and what we need to tell him.'

They disappear down a hole to a warm burrow where Lennie continues his tale.

'It was difficult to get to you, there are many abroad who would do us harm. In the Valley of Ice there has been much activity; a massive black dragon comes and goes, also a very tall black cloaked humanoid, and now Smorkis has returned after months of absence. The Shilocks, ghost like, are everywhere unaffected by the cold. What is going on?'

Caramel says,

'They are guarding a woman down below us in the Ice Palace, it is surrounded by igloos which house the Sylii.'

'The what?' Lennie asks.

'Syllii,' Caramel replies. 'They are the odd-looking creatures that are round with many legs and a body covered in long hair. They have two vicious pincers, and they can extend themselves upwards to become quite tall. With two pairs of wobbly eyes that seem to look everywhere at once, they appear to be perfect jailers. Unlike the Shilocks they are not an invention. We sometimes see the woman out in the garden walking among the ice statues with two Sylli as guards.'

'Can she not just transport herself away?' asks Lennie.

'She must have been robbed of the ability to do that or transmute herself as soon as she was captured. She seems in a drugged state,' says Hannibal. 'We think she is hiding the fact that she is not completely empty as, for a moment, she looked straight at us aware we were watching from up here. Then she smiled the most wonderful smile. We took it as a signal for us to somehow help her; it is difficult to refuse such a contact, thus we thought of the Hermit.'

'Well I think I can take you to him, or at least where he is seen sometimes,' Lennie says, his eyes beginning to close with sleep.

The next day the three Hobis begin their journey. It is arduous, especially when a blizzard blows up and they scurry for shelter in another Hobi warren. The furry ones dodge the roaming groups of Shilocks, the strange creatures that have taken the dragon Smorkis as their leader. That night they lodge with more of their relatives.

The next morning the Hobis are away early, trekking their way over the snowy landscape pushing on as fast as they can. The snow begins to fall again and the day grows dark.

At one-point Lennie who is leading, comes to dead stop before turning, gesturing to the others to run towards a group of black rocks covered in ice. They bury themselves up to their necks in the snow behind the boulders and watch. It is not long before a patrol of Shilocks, their sunken eyes shining like torch beams emerge out of the murk. They seem to be muttering amongst themselves, their sharp beaks opening and shutting. The largest of them suddenly holds up his clawed, sinewy hand and they stop. There are about ten of them. Their leader bends forward as though listening intently looking towards the rocks, looking straight at the Hobis. He points a talon towards them as the snow runs in droplets off his oval, hairless face. They all move towards the rocky outcrop.

'Wait,' whispers Lennie, as the other two get ready to run. 'I don't think they have seen us yet. Get ready, we must go straight through them to carry on the way our path goes.'

The white ghosts get within five metres of the Hobis, when the ground erupts in front of them catching them off guard. The three Hobis are up and running, skidding through the Shilocks, dodging and twisting; only the last one manages to grab Caramel's tail. Hannibal following on bites down hard on its arm and it lets go with a shriek of pain. Very quickly the three are lost to sight against the darkening skies as the snow continues to fall.

Several hours later they arrive at their destination where the weather has settled and the pale sun appears. Exhausted, standing on a ridge they look out on a white plain which has at its centre the warm Lake of Mirramor surrounded by low hills and the tall mountain of Edras. Geysers occasionally blow hot and high into the air, causing a steamy atmosphere to be formed which washes away as the geyser subsides. They have not seen any other creature for some time.

Lennie says, grandly sweeping a paw in an arc,

'The lands of the Hermit and the Ice Maidens.'

'Ice Maidens,' says Hannibal, 'you never mentioned them.'

'Well,' comes the reply, 'they are a legend and I have not met anyone who has actually seen them. Romantic rubbish I expect,' he sniggers.

Caramel says, 'How do we find this man? What

sort of magician is he? Why is he a hermit?'

'Whoa, too many questions,' laughs Lennie. 'The rumour is he lost his lover, the absolute one somehow. They say that she is hidden in the stars and he looks for her endlessly.'

Hannibal snorts at this,

'Sounds like even more romantic tosh to me.'

Lennie continues,

'I think it is likely he will find us. He is sometimes seen on the mountain amongst the petrified trees or fishing in the lake. He is a magician; he will know we are here.'

The three Hobis head for the mountain, picking their way slowly around the hot springs and the shores of the lake. By the time they are on the lower slopes of Mount Edras in the petrified forest, the night's lightshow has started. Digging themselves a shelter of ice and snow, leaving an entrance that looks out over the lake, the weary Hobis climb inside and promptly fall asleep.

Later, in the early hours of the morning, a long silent shadow is cast by the moon over their shelter.

The first streaks of dawn touch the cloudless sky as Lennie creeps out of the ice shelter, rising up on his back legs to his full height to look around. The pale sun starts to create shadows in the frozen trees as below, a geyser belches its hot water into the air. The steam rises to create a mist that wafts up towards him. Joined by Hannibal and Caramel, two other geysers fire off their steamy water covering the trees in a shroud of warm mist.

As the mist clears it reveals a tall lean figure standing watching them with dark slanted eyes, a slight smile playing on his lips. He has a bronzed vibrant face with a long drooping moustache and straight black hair. It flows onto his thick cloak which is clasped together by a brooch of gold shaped like a pair of wings. In his hand he carries a javelin whose finely shaped point is like a prism, rotating slowly, bending the light into different softly glowing colours. A sheath on his back carries a long curved sword.

His voice is soft, yet strong,

'Good morning, I think you are looking for me.'

'Yes, absolutely. Oh, yes that's us, definitely us.' Hannibal starts to gabble until Caramel puts a restraining paw on his shoulder saying,

'Are you the Hermit?'

'I believe that is what I am called, my name is Chingis.'

'And are you a magician?' Chips in Lennie, making the most of this tall man's apparent kindly attitude towards them.

'That word has lots of meanings,' laughs the

Hermit, 'but again I have heard it said.'

Caramel gets straight to the point,

'We have a message, a story for you and we have travelled two days to bring it here.'

'Then we should find somewhere more comfortable where I can hear it.'

He leads them back down through the forest, where long icicles hang from the trees to the shore of the Lake. Climbing up through boulders, they find a terrace where there is a wide fissure in the sheer cliff. He ushers them through the gap into a cave which is lit by a soft luminance coming from several lamps hanging on the cave walls. The cave is warm. In the centre is a stone fireplace with glowing embers; as the Hermit throws on more wood, the smoke rises directly to the high roof and out of some hidden ventilation. There is rush bedding and boxes covered in woven blankets, while at the back of the cave, a stream enters flowing in and out of a small pool. The three Hobis look at the Hermit. They are very thirsty, so he gestures towards the water saying,

'Drink, it's fresh and pure.'

They slake their thirst.

'So, tell me the story.'

Caramel and Hannibal recount the story of the lady with the smile, the Sylii and the tall humanoid. Lennie then tells him of the other comings and goings in the ice valley including the return of the Ice Dragon. The Hermit remains silent, looking serious and thoughtful. They wait for him to say something. He seems to have gone into a trance closing his eyes and sitting very still, until after a short while he opens them again to look directly at the three of them.

'Thank you for bringing this news. I have encountered the Ice Dragon before. I think the prisoner you have found is maybe one of my greatest friends, someone who I have not seen for years. Her name is Rhea. After she and her husband Ambrose disappeared, I left the life of fighting and intrigue. I was tired and wanted to be on my own to study the forces of nature as deeply as I can.

'All the Interventionists were defeated, and those that were left disappeared to lie hidden. I know they still cause trouble trying to reform. They were irritating but were weak. It seems that is changing and something more powerful has replaced them. I heard some rumours of a Darkness, a formless creature.'

He gazes at the Hobis whose faces look mystified.

'Of course, you don't know about these things. This planet has been lost to the Council and not been visited for many years, yet you are the catalyst that may very well change that. Shall I tell you the history, would you like to stay longer my friends?'

The three of them felt drawn in by this man and welcomed a rest before the return journey.

'But don't you want to rush off and rescue your friend,' Caramel said.

'There will be time enough for that fight. Someone is coming, although I think he does not know that at the moment. He will really want to meet you, hear your story and help with a rescue. Let's walk down on the shore.'

They leave the cave and end up sitting on a rock watching the geysers burst against a bright grey sky. The Hermit leans his javelin against a rock where they can watch the prism spin slowly around.

'How do you know someone is coming?' asks Lennie.

'I have the sight. I have the dreamtime.'

'You are a magician then,' says Lennie, happy with establishing that until something else catches his eye in the mist of the geysers.

'What is that coming towards us?' he points along the shoreline.

They turn to look,

'Her name is Persephone,' says the Hermit.

The three Hobi Rats stand shakily up on the rock because looking at them is a white horse with the most beautiful pair of feathered wings. Some way behind her are several others who are also watching them as the geyser mist ebbs and flows around them.

'These are Wind Horses, the so-called Ice Maidens, they ride the winds.'

'B..b..but where do they come from?' stutters Hannibal.

'From the deep past, out of the stars, the frozen wastes and the green valleys. Anywhere and everywhere,' comes the enigmatic reply.

'There isn't a stallion,' says Caramel.

'Oh, there most definitely is one of those. He will come when I call if he chooses to,' says the Magician.

With that he cups his hand to his mouth to let out an eerie high call that echoes down the lake. For a while nothing happens, then there is a dark winged creature, a silhouette in the sun flying towards them coming up over the water. They watch with mouths open as the Wind Horse comes closer, growing in size until it lands to stand magnificent and powerful, pawing the ground.

15: TWO BOATS ON THE SEA

Back on Earth, Bonny spots the red van climbing the mountain road, so sweeping down in front of it she calls to Rodrigo. Immediately pulling over he gets out followed by Spellman as the Eagle comes to perch on the roof of the van. She tells him her terrible news, unbelievable and final. Rodrigo turns to Spellman his eyes blazing,

'She has caught and killed them! Magda Cross's lackey, the Metalion, has killed Sebastian and Lillian. Bonny had no chance of helping them. She says as they died, they transmuted back and are lying at the bottom of a cliff.'

Spellman immediately asks,

'And where is Willow?'

'After checking on Sebastian and Lillian and realising there was nothing she could do for them, Bonny flew up again to find Willow was missing. Only Dynasta was there with another of his kind celebrating his cowardly act.'

The two Protectors look at each other knowing what is coming next. Two young people whose lives have already changed immeasurably need to be told the dreadful news.

Spellman says, his voice gruff and low,

'Sebastian and Lillian will not be lost to us by this, they will travel with us. Retribution will follow this monster. Dynasta will be mine.'

The two Protectors look at each other as the awful shock begins to settle into them. They clasp hands supporting each other before getting into the van to turn it around.

'I wonder where Willow will have got to this time. She must be terrified,' Spellman says.

'Yes,' Rodrigo replies. 'It looks as though Sebastian and Lillian were trying to buy time for her to escape from Dynasta. I guess she has run off into the woods. Bonny has gone back to look for her.'

At the farm Lottie is watching Branca show Christine some moves with the sword. She is learning fast, her red hair streaming as she whirls and feints to try to get close in. Sergio and Jack are out on the mountain not far away walking the sheep with the dogs, making the most of the sunny weather. The red van pulls into the yard. The two fighters stop to watch Rodrigo and Spellman get out of the truck their faces serious and sad.

'You're back quickly,' calls Christine.

Lottie, remembering her vision of the morning says to herself quietly,

'Oh, here it comes.'

'Let's go inside,' Spellman says to Christine and Branca.

Rodrigo walks across to Lottie. She doesn't move but sees the stress on his face.

'I have terrible news,' he says. 'There is no easy way to say it, Sebastian and Lillian are dead. Magda Cross has killed them or at least caused it to happen.'

For a few moments Lottie's shoulders slump, her head bows, eyes closed as his words slam into her. She clenches her fists tightly then looks up managing to whisper,

'How?'

'Bonny arrived just as the two off them were falling down a sheer cliff face. The Metalion Dynasta and another then pushed the Land Rover over the cliff. When Bonny got there they were both already dead. They must have fought the Metalions to protect Willow who seems to have escaped. We don't know where she is, Bonny is looking for her.'

Lottie still clenching her fists draws into herself, trying to sort out in her mind what she has just heard. She sends a message out, more a cry for help to Jack.

Five minutes later her brother is walking

through the trees to see his sister sat at the table with Rodrigo, their heads are bowed in silence. Both look up at the sound of his approach, their faces serious edged with grief. Lottie immediately gets to her feet while Rodrigo looks grimly at Jack as he walks away towards the house to join the others.

'What's up?' Jack asks.

'Sebastian and Lillian are dead killed by that metal creature summoned by Magda Cross,' Lottie blurts out.

Jack stares at her saying the first thing that comes into his head,

'But they were here this morning, just a few hours ago.'

'I know,' she says gently, 'let's sit down.'

Jack sits opposite her. Looking at each other, holding hands across the wooden board the shock comes in waves. They try to speak, although words are there they make no sound. Rocking gently backwards and forwards struggling to accept what has happened, the pain and loss washes over them, yet no tears will come.

Eventually Jack says, his voice brittle and quiet,

'How did they die?'

Lottie breathes in and out deeply, then slowly, quietly she tells him.

They take little notice of Sergio arriving back with the sheep, Meg and Tess running around keeping them together in a group. Christine is out of the house quickly to help put them in the barn and let him know the news.

Jack is beginning to rage. Lottie watches it rising like a fire catching hold.

'Not now,' she says to him. 'Now is not the time. First, we tend to the two that raised us and kept us safe. We will be strong, she will not win, we will take them with us and we will celebrate their lives even as we cry for their passing.'

Jack nods his head, the sunlight for a moment touching his fair hair.

'Yes,' is all he says.

After a while Rodrigo comes out of the house walking towards them.

'We need to go and get Sebastian and Lillian,' he says quietly.

Jack stands up ready to go.

'Not you Jack. The police will be there by now. There will be much talking to be done and I think for now, you and Lottie should let Christine and I handle it. It will seem an obvious accident. Here funerals take place quickly, usually within days. You will both have to sign papers but I think it is possible for me to get the bodies released to us directly.'

Jack is unsure but Lottie says,

'I think that is wise Jack. We should accept that kind offer.'

The others come out of the house to group around them, their faces drawn and sad. Everyone has tears in their eyes.

'No,' says Jack looking around his eyes hard, his voice fighting for control. 'Lottie is right, now is not the time to cry. There are things to be done first. Soon we will mourn them, then we will catch those that killed them and destroy what they stand for.'

There is a pause, a nodding of heads, then they step forward to hug one another drawing whatever strength they can.

Several days have passed. Shades watch from the shadows; the wolves and the Wild Ones are there in the cover of the bushes and trees. The leave taking and the grief wine is bitter in the mouths of the mourners as they toast the lives of Lillian and Sebastian.

Light crackles on the horizon as the warm sun, dropping red, shapes the clouds like a pair of dragons rising. The two wooden boats with small sails are rolling gently against the rocks in the lonely inlet. The Mediterranean Sea is calm although a gentle breeze blows offshore. Lillian and Sebastian lie one in each covered in flowers. Jack and Lottie stand alone on the shore saying farewell.

They tie the boats together, then push them out on the offshore swell as the breeze rises to fill the sails. All eyes are fixed on the little craft as everyone says their personal farewells, talking to their own gods, committing Sebastian and Lillian to memory as the boats get into the receding tide. Soon they become smaller sailing out on the wide expanse of water. Just for a moment they do an odd thing, spinning slowly around as though looking back before straightening out to edge closer to the horizon.

As he looks out to sea, his face taut with grief, into Jack's head comes the vision of the Lady with the smile. She is staring at him intently.

The boats are nearly lost from sight, when in the distant sky out at sea, a dim shape flanked by two smaller ones come into view. They seem to hover for a moment, then there are three bursts of flame, and the boats are left to burn and sink as the three dragons disappear.

Rodrigo comes to stand by Lottie who, shocked by the finality of it whispers to him,

'Is that really it? All there is?'

'What there is now,' he says looking at her, 'is the comfort of what they have left in our memory and we have our friendship. We hold onto that. They travel with us. We will always be saying their names.'

117

Jack's sadness and feeling of loss is gradually being replaced with anger and fury that begins to steadily pump through him. He concentrates on the face that welcomes him with her smile, whose eyes now see him, calling for him. Then the force comes; he begins to feel light, like being caught up in a strong but gentle wind as it lifts him away.

After a while of staring at the empty sea, Lottie turns to look back towards Jack but there is an empty space.

'Where's Jack? Where has he gone?' she cries out.

There is still no sign of Willow.

16: AGNES WITH THE SISTERS OF THE NIGHT

In the city of Menos on the principle planet of Alpha, Adeth leader of the Council is meeting with Darius, popular hero, great friend of Ambrose and with Rodrigo. The grief is plainly written on the latter's face as he tells them what has happened to Sebastion and Lillian.

'We have been friends for so long, fought so many battles together alongside Ambrose and Rhea, it is a terrible shock,' Adeth says shaking his head sadly. 'I am afraid there will be more losses to come while our enemies are secretly growing. What was once hidden continues to rise, like those experimental beings the Metalions appearing in different places. The Darkness, which we have seen bleeds into them all a black joy of evil power, is getting stronger and seems untouchable.

'Their attacks appear to be deliberately random to keep us guessing. Yet I think there could be someone or something else orchestrating all this. Someone focussed on destroying centuries of learning and study, and non-involvement in other worlds or their development. Another source that may be hidden, perhaps even among us in Menos.'

'Yes maybe,' says Darius angrily. 'We have said this many times, but I urge we take stronger actions to counter what is happening. We need to publicise the need to watch ourselves carefully, to report all unusual activity, to in effect spy on ourselves to kill off those who would do us harm.'

'That would have to be carefully handled; trust and support for each other has always been our way. Our very nature has been diversity, logic and understanding,' Rodrigo replies.

'I know it Brother but we cannot wait to be led into chaos.'

Meanwhile on Earth, one of their enemies Magda Cross is happy, her boy, her new 'son' sleeps soundlessly, hidden away while his doting Mother watches over him like a hawk.

'This time no one will take my son from me,' she tells the Harlequin who simply smiles as she continues. 'The plan to inflict pain and reduce those opposing us worked perfectly. Now another bigger scheme is taking place as we speak, that will bring the Twins into our hands.'

She has ordered all her grim associates to disappear for a while following the deaths of Sebastian and Lillian. She tells them she will call them back very soon when the time is ready to strike again.

That night Agnes and the Sisters find Willow wandering aimlessly under cover of the forest, occasionally stopping to sit by a tree. She looks thin, hungry and dirty. Every now and then, as they watched and followed her, she would hit her head against a tree and moan, crying and pulling at her hair, arguing with herself. They can hear her whispering the names of Sebastian and Lillian as though calling to them in secret. The hooded shadows stay silent.

Agnes the earthbound Witch is being very careful, intent on keeping away from Magda Cross, even her witchy sisters did not know where she was hiding. The previous summer she had been recruited by the lies of Miss Cross, then realising the extent of the damage and hurt that was being proposed, changed sides becoming a friend to Lottie. Not something that the wicked one would forgive.

When Agnes found out that Magda Cross the Chimera and Cravenclaw were back she thought it best to disappear for a while. Eda took her into the caves behind the waterfall. The Sisters have much in common with the Wild Ones.

Agnes knows that the girl they are currently tracking is being sought, although this is a Willow that she does not recognise, so different from the brave confident person she saw last. Deciding to show herself, she carefully approaches the young woman as the other Sisters stay hidden.

'Willow,' she calls gently, 'what has happened to you?'

Willow jumps up startled and looks hard at Agnes, her face blotchy, red and streaked with tears. She is ready to run, then a look of recognition comes into her eyes and she starts to sob uncontrollably.

'Oh, come on my dear, sit down here again and tell me what's happened,' says Agnes, drawing back her hood to reveal her beautiful steel grey hair.

Eventually, Willow starts to sob the story out, beginning with her disappearance and the time with the Demon, to the death of Sebastian and Lillian. The Sisters come out of the dark to draw closer around her forming a bond of sympathy.

'I didn't know what to do. I hid and heard the Land Rover go over the cliff. When Dynasta was gone I crept back to peep over the edge from the undergrowth and saw them both lying there. I ran into the wood to hide and now I cannot face the others. I can't believe they are dead.'

'Shush,' says Agnes, 'I am sure they are all very worried about you. You must come with us now and we will take you back to them.'

They help her up and she lets them lead her through the forest, leaning heavily on a Sister's arm until they see the road they must cross. Going quietly to ground they watch to see if it is safe to move into the open.

Agnes suddenly becomes aware that the forest has grown quiet. The sounds of the night creatures have died away, no screech of an owl nor call of a fox or the rustling of small creatures. She sees a deer a little way off standing rigid, then she sees why.

At the forest edge on the other side of the road is a huge horse, a black dog and a rider wrapped in a cloak, still as a statue. Willow, catching sight of the Demon is about to scream, when she is grabbed, a hand going quickly over her mouth. The dog's ears prick up and it moves towards the edge of the wood followed by the Demon. He leans over his horse's neck searching the shadows for any sight of the girl.

'Willow, Willow,' comes the quiet urgent voice of the cloaked figure. 'Remember you are mine. I am here for you. Come to me.'

The Sisters melt back into the wood moving quickly away from the Demon holding tightly onto the girl, who in the dark of the forest remembers and smiles to herself, a smile of pure malice.

The others take her further on, while Agnes drawing her long knife waits hidden in the bushes to watch expecting to see who follows. The pathways stay empty, nothing comes after them. Her eyes glitter in the dark, there is something odd here. She sheaths her knife and follows the others until they meet up outside her old dwelling by the river which is an obvious place to search. Staying just long enough to grab a warm cloak and some dry biscuits and water for Willow, they head further on for a clearing in the trees which is at the end of a rough wide track.

While the others hide themselves away Agnes walks into the centre of the clearing and calls out, mimicking an eagle cry perfectly. An answer comes almost at once. She walks back to say to Willow,

'They know where we are now. Spellman will come for you soon. I think though a little more protection won't hurt.' She utters a low wolf bark several times.

There isn't an answer although soon they see the eyes that are suddenly watching them, as the grey shapes also settle to wait out the night.

Half an hour away, Magda Cross breathes out a sigh of satisfaction at the success of her evil plan.

'They are on their way,' she says to Naptha the Demon. 'They think you still want her back, and she doesn't have to act scared because she is.'

Naptha regards the woman standing in front of him and says seriously,

'Oh, but I do want her back eventually.'

The sky lightens and the sun's rays begin to streak across the sky as Agnes hears the noise of a truck on the track. The grey brothers and sisters disappear as the powerful Mitsubishi swings into the clearing, coming to a stop to let Spellman and Branca jump out. Christine immediately starts to turn the vehicle around. Spellman rushes to gather Willow up, calling his thanks to Agnes and the Sisters who are standing watching from the trees. Branca and Agnes shake hands and introduce themselves.

'Was it you that called Bonny?' Branca asks.

'Oh yes,' says Agnes, 'and the grey ones too.'

Branca smiles at her,

'You have some knowledge Sister. We should talk together sometime soon.'

Agnes shrugs and returns the smile,

'I know the hidden and secret names for some things,' she says. 'However, there is something wrong here Branca. Willow is greatly changed and shocked, but why weren't we followed last night if Naptha is so keen to have her back? He had a dog that could have tracked us which I waited to kill. Yet it did not come, and I wonder why not?'

'Mm,' mused Branca. 'Why indeed? I will keep a careful watch and speak to Rodrigo.'

'Come on! We need to get going,' Spellman

shouts.

Soon the truck is on its way back.

17: WHERE DRAGONS MEET

'I am lost. What is this place?' Jack is thinking as he shivers and draws his cloak tighter around himself. Having managed to transport himself, his excitement is tempered by the cold winter landscape. In front of him is a village of igloos dominated by an Ice Palace. Turning to look around, he sees the white wastelands sloping upwards towards higher ground, above which loom high icy cliffs. The rest of the landscape is a bleak snowy plain on which the weak, watery sun shines bringing little warmth.

'Where is the woman who calls me?' He asks himself as a feeling of great danger comes to him.

Jack becomes aware that a strange creature, almost invisible against the snow is watching him. Tall, with a pale moon face, a wicked looking beak and deep eye sockets, it points one of its long talons at him and chatters loudly. Immediately another appears and then another; soon there are twenty of them. He backs away as the Shilocks move menacingly forward trying to encircle him.

The air shifts, going out of focus to reveal the Great Grey Wolf, angry and savage, his teeth bared growling at them. Briefly, it brings them to a halt as other Shilocks appear to help capture this unusual prize.

Quickly realising he has little chance the Wolf turns to run fast for the high ground taking one of the many tracks that crisscross it. Catching the Shilocks by surprise it gives him a head start to climb higher as they begin to follow him. Running hard the Wolf rounds a bend to come face to face with a furry, black and white rat-like creature standing up on his hind legs. Holding up a paw, he stops Jack just long enough to say,

'This way, we have been waiting for you.'

The Hobi dives off the track and into the white rock-strewn landscape he knows well. There are so many ways to go but they move surely and swiftly. Jack doesn't hesitate to follow as they race around boulders and rocky outcrops, soon losing their pursuers. Pressing on without speaking, they keep up the pace until eventually the Hobi slows down and stops beneath a large frozen tree. He looks up at the Wolf grinning and says,

'Well that was fun. Please allow me to introduce myself. My name is Lennie and I am pleased to make your acquaintance.'

Jack, whose head is spinning with the sudden

strangeness of it all transmutes back.

Lennie watches as the air seems to go unfocused around the Wolf revealing a human being, a tall fair-haired youth is looking at him.

'Whoa neat trick!' The furry one exclaims, 'I saw you do that just now, very impressive.'

'Hello,' Jack says feeling silly, 'I am Jack from Earth.'

'Oh, I know who you are. You are now on the Winter Planet in the Galaxy of Horizon. We Hobis have been watching for you. The Hermit gave us the word that you would come.'

'Who is this Hermit and how did he know I was coming?'

'Ah, I can answer the first question but haven't a clue with the second. However, we don't have much time, those Shilocks will be tracking us and the night is only a few hours away. It also looks like another blizzard is coming,' he points to the heavy grey clouds gathering in the distance. 'There is a warm place waiting for us tonight, after that we will need to move swiftly onwards to meet the Hermit, although really he is a magician. We will have plenty of time to talk tonight.'

Jack, warming to this irrepressible creature just says,

'Ok, you're the leader.'

Away they go, the Wolf reappearing again to use

his better camouflage and speed.

Making good time with no mishaps, they arrive several hours later at another small mountain to be greeted by other Hobis. They are shown to a small cave where they find warm downy feathered blankets and nuts, dried fruit and fresh water. The storytelling starts as they make themselves comfortable with the wind rising to become a blizzard of snow and ice. Eventually sleep overtakes them both, Jack smiles as he falls asleep noting that Hobis have a very comforting snore.

The pale-yellow dawn breaks with Lennie up and about early as usual, finding the blizzard has gone leaving the day bright and clear. The Hobi looks across a flat plain bisected by a frozen river to see another mountain range he recognises. The ice valley, where he watched the coming and goings of the Ice Dragon lies there. The mountains rise to sharp peaks, and he can see the sun glinting off the frozen waterfalls of ice cascading down them. Several other Hobis come up to him pointing across the snowy plain at a large flying creature, the sunlight sparkling off its great bulk.

'Smorkis,' he says.

'Did you say Smorkis?' asks Jack coming up behind them.

'Yes, the Ice Dragon,' answers Lennie. 'A creature that's worth keeping as far away from as possible, although I wonder what she is up to and where she is heading. She has only recently returned.'

'Mm,' Jack mutters, not really interested until one of the Hobis says,

'She often meets with another black dragon even bigger than she is.'

Jack swivels around,

'What was that, did you say a black dragon?'

'Yes, a huge creature; we don't know where it came from.'

'Oh, I think I do,' Jack replies.

Lennie says,

'These ones tell me they avoid that place as much as possible. There is a darkness that occasionally swirls around it that has not been here before and certainly does not bode well for any of us.'

'Oh, and I know about that too.'

They watch as Smorkis flies into the largest valley that they can see.

'I think we should go on a little recce.' Jack says.

Lennie looks a bit dubious about that, pointing and saying,

'My cousins here tell me strange things happen over there.'

Jack is insistent. The death of his 'earth' parents has brought him immeasurable grief and anger, but their courage has strengthened him. He knows what they would do. For a moment he looks to the horizon seeing their faces.

'I am on my road now,' he whispers to himself, 'wherever it goes, whatever I find.'

Lennie looking at him, sees the determined look,

'C'mon,' he says. 'Let's go quickly then.'

Jack changes, and the Great Grey Wolf with his companion make their way across the plain using whatever cover they can find.

Inside the valley a meeting of the unlovely is happening. Surrounding them is an open-air cathedral of ice. The ground is covered in soft snow and there are ice bridges between rock faces from which large spears of ice hang, and frozen waterfalls cascade into an iced, still river that meanders across the plain. The Chimera Magda Cross stands on a large ice platform slightly higher than the two dragons Smorkis and Cravenclaw, her two heads regarding them both. Surrounding them are fire points, flames issuing from the ground like bushes of fire, very hot but leaving no impression on the frozen land. Many Shilocks, impervious to the cold, servants to the dragon Smorkis, huddle closer to hear what is being said.

Having managed to creep into the valley without being detected, the Wolf and the Hobi watch the meeting from a distance. They cannot get closer for fear of being seen and caught.

Suddenly the light seems to fade as the Darkness comes to meet its disciples, descending and swirling about the Chimera and the two dragons obscuring the watchers' view. The Darkness increases whirling around between the fires, and then suddenly from the depth of its shadows there appears a massive Humanoid in a long black robe with a large hood. The three creatures bow their heads briefly, the Shilocks drop to their knees. The Darkness recedes and flows around low over the ground as the Humanoid raises its arms as though in welcome. Their Lord and Master has come, and it seems all are touched by his black joy and his insanity.

However, there is a pause and the hooded head turns to look around; he feels that all is not as it should be. There is another presence here. Immediately the Wolf feels the danger and starts to back away followed by Lennie; they creep around a corner to run silent and fast across the plain. Jack realises they have little chance of escape as they are completely exposed and in the open, unless he leaves Lennie and transports back to Earth he will be caught.

Just as he is thinking he cannot leave the Hobi, Lennie panting and puffing shouts,

'Go!' You must get away!'

'I can't do that.'

'You have to go,' Lennie says again.

Jack looks back and can see the two enormous dragons, wings beating taking to the sky.

Out of nowhere comes a movement of the air like a rushing wind. Suddenly, running beside them, is a black winged stallion carrying a tall rider in a long thick coat, holding a javelin with a prism of rotating light at its end. On the other side, a stunning white winged mare gallops, easily keeping pace with them. The rider turns and points the javelin behind them, lightning crackles from it and the sky goes dark and heavy as a shroud of snow starts to fall obscuring them from view.

In a demonstration of superb riding skills, the horseman leans over and grabs Lennie with his other hand, who makes an undignified squeak. He shouts at the Wolf to get on the white horse. The pace slows down as Jack transmutes back with Persephone coming to a standstill. Grabbing her mane, he scrabbles up onto her back as she sets off again picking up speed, to rise through the snow into the sky and away. Jack cannot help himself; he laughs and shouts with relief, feeling an incredible sense of pure freedom and utter amazement.

After what seems a short while the Lake of Mirramor comes into view, and with it the land of geysers, the frozen forest and the mountain of Edras. There the story will be told again, this time to the son of the woman held captive.

18: MOMENTS OF DOUBT AND PAIN

In Spain several days have passed. After the funeral there is a listless and sombre feeling amongst them all, it is difficult to find any energy. A tall bearded man is standing by himself high on the mountainside, part warrior, part mystic and part motor mechanic. He is drawn there by his own dreams, and for several hours has been looking over a deep ice cold lake, lost in thought as the night comes on. The man can see from where he sits the waves of mountains rolling away to the Mediterranean Sea under a brilliant starlit sky. The tree line is some metres away whispering in the light breeze, for once he is totally alone.

He has lost the brother and sister-in-law he loves but cannot find. He also thinks he has lost two of his greatest friends forever after failing to protect them from the evil force. He is now hunted by the Black Dragon Paedrenostra. His guardianship of his nephew and niece is wavering particularly as his nephew has just gone missing.

He wonders if his wisdom, intellect and valour are being called into question and found wanting.

Rodrigo is looking for some moments of peace and solitude so he can reach out to touch reality and purpose within himself. His dreams are filled with the image of the great tree growing in the desert under its panoply of colourful stars. Flashes of light come mixed with the images of dragon fire. Rhea's face is there caught up with images of Sebastian and Lillian. Strange echoes are calling him from the unfathomable music and mysteries of the ever-expanding Universe, making his purpose, his very being seem insignificant.

A watcher slithers through the trees towards him, she cannot believe her good luck to find him on his own yet again. She salivates at the thought of catching him and what she will do to him. Her revenge on the Protectors she killed the last time he escaped her clutches means nothing against having him in her power.

Paedrenostra's eyes are slits, as her long body moves silently from side to side until she arrives at the edge of the wood.

'Carefully now,' she hisses quietly to herself as she curls herself up ready to spring out on her enemy. She now knows how dangerous this human can be.

'Rodrigo,' calls Branca as she comes out of the trees towards him. The She-Dragon goes to ground her tongue flicking out hissing softly.

'I wondered where you had gone Brother. You have been missing for quite a while. Shall I leave you alone?'

Rodrigo breathes in deeply and turns to look at her worried face framed by her short luxuriant black hair. He shrugs and says,

'I am struggling Sister.'

She reaches up to grasp his shoulders, to bend him down towards her so that their foreheads touch. His hands hold her shoulders and they press their heads together tightly. An energy flows, strength and friendship renewing, electric emotion like lightning sparks between them making them shake slightly, and it binds them together.

They break apart, as she says,

'All is one, you are not alone. We are all together.'

He nods and smiles,

'I know it perhaps more than most but sometimes my strength ebbs a little.'

He is about to say more when he sees what is behind her, black and fiery, her wings lifting her from the ground. Everything speeds up. He pushes Branca away so hard, that unprepared, she almost flies through the air to neatly roll over and be up onto her knees.

Ignoring Branca, Paedrenostra stops in front of Rodrigo who has no time to change. Towering over him on her back legs she breathes over him, freezing him so that he is unable to move. She hisses,

'You think I am just going to kill you? You will beg me for that. Only when I am tired of you will I consider it.'

She lowers her great black head to stare into his eyes, hoping to see fear and panic. For a moment her attention is drawn by a flap of birdspeed coming across the lake towards her. Bonnie flies straight at her, only veering away at the last moment as a gout of fire issues from the She-Dragon to warm the night air. Branca is also running towards her throwing her axe as she moves; it is an accurate throw that hits the Dragon on her snout. The weapon spins away without doing any damage. Paedrenostra turns to move crocodile-like towards the Shield Maiden.

The Black Dragon is low and fast over the ground, her jaws wide and deadly. Suddenly she is met full on by Ironjaw as the Great Red Dragon materialises to drift in from the night sky. The two enormous Dragons don't hesitate, but smash into each other snarling and biting. Paedrenostra's long sinewy body curls around the Red Dragon to hold tight with her claws, trying to bite into Ironjaw's neck as he rises in the air in an effort to shake her off. Suddenly he drops like a stone, hitting the ground and rolling over on top of the Black One. Over they go several times before they hit the trees with such force that it uproots some of them.

Branca with great daring follows the fight as closely as she can trying to use her sword, an almost impossible task in the melee of teeth and claws. Picking up her axe she waits until there is a single clear moment where there is a slight gap between them. Throwing it with all her strength, it whistles through the air to prick the corner of the Black Dragon's eye making her shake her head in anger. In doing so she loosens her grip on Ironjaw long enough for him to bite down hard into one of her front legs.

Paedrenostra turns swiftly as the blood gushes out gathering all her strength to slither towards the lake, her three good legs propelling her as fast as they can. In a moment she is in the water and disappearing beneath its surface. Ironjaw arrives seconds later, but the waters of the lake ripple and flow covering the Black Dragon's escape.

Branca is bent over Rodrigo who has fallen to the ground not moving, staring sightlessly at the sky. She stands up as Ironjaw comes to blow his healing breath over his fellow Protector and great friend. Bonnie perched in a tree, watches as Rodrigo helped up by Branca recovers to be gently admonished by Ironjaw.

'Brother you cannot walk alone now. This one,' he nods towards the lake, 'is gone now but she is not finished, especially now she has found you again. Until she is killed you will not be safe.'

'Thank you, Brother, at least she is wounded,' Rodrigo says, shaking his head gently to clear it.

'It will easily repair, she will be back, you must be on your guard.'

'How did you find us? 'Branca asks.

'I have come to meet Lottie and was directed this way,' Ironjaw says enigmatically.

Branca replies,

'Lottie went with Eda and Agnes to a hideaway place for a while. We are trying to give her some peace to help her recover from losing her earth parents.'

'No matter, she knows I am here, but I think it is urgent that we move on now, Sebastian and Lillian would know that.'

'Ah, yes in that regard,' says Branca to them both, 'we need to find out about Willow. Spellman, lovely fellow that he is, will not have a word said against her but something is wrong.'

'Then we need to meet with him and discuss it,' says Rodrigo as they leave the clearing.

There is lightness under one of the trees, faint but definite, watching as they go. The Gatekeeper of the Light, her tattooed face looking even older smiles grimly, her hand on the Sword of Light, her back bent, her cloak interweaving with the colours of the rainbow.

19: A TRAP IS SET

Willow, living at Christine's with the others keeps calling for Jack. Although he is not there she continues to whine and begs to see him. They keep her close, particularly Spellman who constantly tries to reach her, sitting with her telling tales of their adventures together. He reminds her of her status as a Protector, and walking with her in the warm early spring sunshine tries to draw out the old Willow. Christine and Sergio carry on with the workings of the farm, always making sure there are two of them walking the sheep. They try to take her with them, something she loved to do, enjoying the wild country and the sense of freedom it offers but she becomes sullen and refuses.

Branca, Rodrigo and Spellman gather together, trying to decide what to do to end her torment. The Shield Maiden is forthright and comes straight to the point telling Spellman what Agnes said about not being followed.

Spellman shakes his head.

'It proves nothing; there could be many reasons why Agnes and her Sisters weren't followed.'

'But,' argues Branca, 'she does none of the things she is famous for. Where is that beautiful voice? Where is the soft glow that she can make? Where is the brave little mouse that is her alter self who seems to have disappeared, yet she told us when she escaped the first time the mouse was still in her?

'Naptha the Demon robbed her of those things. We know that. She needs time and care,' comes the reply.

Rodrigo says gently,

'That maybe Brother but Branca is right. Remember she told us when she first came to us on that foul and wet night, that she escaped capture by changing. Why wasn't she doing that after escaping from the Land Rover?'

Spellman the warrior pauses before replying, his black face screwed up with worry and concern.

'I can't answer that,' he says. 'We will have to ask her.'

Rodrigo says carefully, aware of Spellman's care and love for his ward,

'Branca and I have another thought. We think she may have been turned by the Demon, not just painfully emptied of her being before she got to us. The whole escape thing is a nonsense, not once, but twice. She has crossed to the Darkness. She is their puppet.'

143

Spellman interrupts savagely,

'You are saying she is a spy. She would rather die
than be that.'

Branca says quietly, her face serious and worried,

'She may not have had that choice. They want
her alive now and the Demon is cruel. He will have
been extremely hard on her.'

Spellman shakes his head again but says nothing.

Rodrigo says urgently to his comrade,

'We have to find out if that's true. If it is, then we
must try and rescue her. You must see that.'

Spellman looks at them both, two of the people
he trusts most, and nods his head reluctantly saying,

'How?'

Two nights later it is a cold starry night, lit with
a half-moon which brings shadows of the trees
across the track. Some way down from the farmhouse Naptha waits astride his horse, the black
dog at his side. He is patient, listening intently, his
strange piercing blue eyes watching until he spots
a slim figure moving quickly along the verge.

'I am here,' he whispers, a sound hardly more
than a breath; she hears it and smiles wickedly as
she moves towards him. The black dog sits down

watching her.

'I have news of Jack,' she says, 'they have lost him. He seems to have had a breakdown after the deaths of Sebastian and Lillian. Presumably he is wandering somewhere across these mountains. They seek him but he has not yet been found.'

'Ah, then we should help them with that search,' he grins. 'Are you safely back with them and do they trust you?'

'Oh yes, they worry about me but that is all.'

'Good,' comes the reply. 'You did well to get those other two to turn into the clearing but there is much yet to do.'

The Demon looks at her, blue eyes flaring, his face changed to a deep shade of red. His voice rises slightly,

'You are mine, and if you want to survive be sure to stay that way.'

Willow recoils terrified.

'Now go back,' she is commanded.

She quickly slides away, while the Demon looks around before moving slowly down the track to his horse.

As the muffled hoof-beats clump quietly down the track, the two watchers Eda and Rezto rise slowly up from the undergrowth. They wait until they are sure Willow will be back inside the Farmhouse, and then they make their way to the barn to wake Rodrigo.

The next day dawns with the sun shining on Rodrigo, Spellman and Branca who are meeting outside to decide what to do.

Spellman is shocked and worried. He is an action man, a fighter with extraordinary skills, but this change in Willow that brought about such traitorous behaviour has left him at a loss to find a solution, other than seeking revenge against those that are the cause of Willow's pain.

He looks at the other two.

'How could she conspire to kill our friends, people she cared about deeply?'

Rodrigo says to him,

'Brother, this is not Willow. She is not the brave fearless person that entered the nest of the giant centipedes the Tigari, or crept into Cravenclaw's cave to find the stolen boy and then faced up to the black dragon. She has been completely brainwashed and something has been put into her mind that celebrates evil.'

Branca adds,

'I imagine she is also really frightened of herself, of what she has become, and of the Demon and Magda Cross who did this. We must bring her back somehow. We have to hope there is something of the person we love left hidden deep within her.'

'Dragon breath!' exclaims Spellman. 'Get Iron-jaw to breathe over her.'

Rodrigo smiles grimly,

'Indeed, the magic of the red dragons can have a part to play but it is deeper than that, they will have set up a guard within her against the obvious. We need to find Lottie, Agnes and Eda.'

Branca and Rodrigo look at each other and she says simply,

'Where there is dark the light will follow.'

'It is her only chance,' says Rodrigo, 'but first, what is in her needs to know we are aware of it and we are coming to get it. I will find the others then we will set up a meeting.'

That evening after dark Ironjaw silently turns up as Rodrigo gathers all those at the farm to-gether. He tells them of the fight that he and Branca had with Paedrenostra. As they all begin to talk about it, the great dragon lowers his head to look at Willow, his fierce eyes turning softer,

'Willow,' he says in his deep voice. 'Good to see you but you look really unwell.'

'Oh, I am alright,' Willow says assuming a sim-pering tone and a pose of someone who has had to put up with a lot.

'I was captured but I escaped. I have been very brave but these ones,' she waves a finger vaguely in the direction of Rodrigo and Branca, 'don't understand what I have been through.'

'You are not what you pretend,' Rodrigo thunders at her. 'You cannot deny it. You were heard last night talking to that wretch Naptha. You helped them to kill Sebastian and Lillian!'

She whirls around to stare at him.

'We set a trap for you,' Rodrigo continues,' with information that is only partly true to see what you would do with it, and you went as soon as possible to the Demon.'

Willow's face changes and becomes full of loathing and malice as she hisses and spits out like a cat.

'You know nothing. You are finished. I will watch them destroy you,' she laughs loudly. 'You can't touch me, my Master will come to take me.'

As she looks wildly around for somewhere to run, Ironjaw blows a deep breath like a warm wind all over her; she staggers and would have fallen but Rodrigo grabs her. It is as though she has been hypnotised, just staring blankly at them.

The Red Dragon shakes his great head sadly,

'She will be like that for a quite a while.'

Spellman, shocked and worried helps carry Willow to the red van.

As he starts to get in Rodrigo says,

'No, my friend this is shocking enough, I think

you should stay here. We will let you know straight away what happens to her. We will look after her.'

Spellman allows himself to be gently pulled away by Christine.

20: WRIGGLEY WORM

Rodrigo and Branca drive their fellow Protector up the road for several kilometres then along a rough track to find a place to park up and lift her out. They carry her through the mountain scrubland for some time into a wooded valley, a place hardly visited by humankind. As the trees get thicker it is more difficult to find a way, until two Wild Ones Treeborn and Dorcas appear. They lead them on various secret paths for several more kilometres until they reach the glade where the river waterfalls down a sheer rock face.

Lottie has made her own way to the cave. Others are also gathered here, more of the Wild Ones and the Sisters of the Night making a small crowd of well-wishers who part to let them through as Eda appears. He leads them behind the waterfall.

The cave system is massive and deep. Beyond the small entrance cave, it spreads out into large caverns where the Wild Ones have built many of their dwellings. Lit by light from natural ventilation shafts and huge burning torches it is Eda's primary hideout. Lottie has been in this cave complex several times so she leads them into a special candlelit cave followed by Agnes.

Willow is laid on a large stone slab. The roof and walls are sparkling with tiny points of light picked up in the candlelight, although more intriguing, are four rectangles of a light-coloured substance about a metre by a half wide which emanates a very feint luminance. Eda explains,

'These little ones are diamonds,' he says. 'However, we have no idea what the others are even though we have been in this region for over a thousand years, they were here before us.'

Lottie stands at the head of the slab looking at Willow lying there not moving, her eyes open but unfocused. The twins and Willow had become remarkably close in such a brief time. Now Lottie is torn by what she has heard of Willow's part in her earth parents' death. It is even more difficult because she still cannot contact Jack, doesn't know where he is and feels he is not close by.

Willow's beautiful face has lost its cunning screwed up look to become serene again, making it hard to forget how much this brave young Protector helped them. It adds to Lottie's confusion, it will be difficult to forgive her actions even if they can save her.

Rodrigo, Branca, Eda, his wife Rhaina with some of the elder Wild Ones gather around Willow with Agnes and her Sisters. Everybody grows quiet and still, the atmosphere becoming charged with emotion as their thoughts concentrate on the lost girl. Rodrigo raises his arms and begins to chant the 'Life'.

Who sees the dawn's rays?

Who feels the sun's warmth?

Who welcomes the day?

Where is the seeker?

What is to be found?

You rise now

Or you will drown.

You make the choices

You catch the breeze,

Hold onto the life seed

That you most need

What will you become?

Clear your mind

Leave that which binds,

Rage and shout.

You are the one!

You are one!

Come on out!

Rodrigo, with the others joining in repeats it over and over his voice strong and deep. Rhaina begins to sing, her voice vibrant above the monotony of the chanting. She sings a song of the wild, it echoes haunting the recesses of the cave. Those that have the dreamtime concentrate on trying to find the girl lying inert on the solid rock.

Lottie is still, letting her mind wander yet concentrating. Vague pictures start to form in her mind as her brain begins to do the now familiar shift. As the images strengthen, she finds herself on a seashore where the sand is turning to an oozing mud as it enters the water. The tide is coming in rapidly towards Willow who, stuck fast in the shallows waves her arms frantically above her head. She is calling out yet makes no sound, her eyes beseeching Lottie to rescue her as she flails about.

'What is in here?' Lottie asks herself as she moves towards Willow stepping into the edge of the sucking mud.

Immediately a myriad of long, white, wriggling mud worms rise to the surface causing the mud to boil in front of the trapped girl. Their sharp little teeth snap open and shut ready to bite anyone coming close to their prisoner. Willow her face contorted with the strain, is fighting to keep herself above the ooze as the sea comes ever closer.

Lottie's brain begins to whirl; images arrive of

Magda Cross, Cravenclaw, the Darkness and most of all the Demon who set this curse which holds its victim so tightly. For a moment she hesitates as her grief for Sebastian and Lillian comes flooding back. She could leave Willow to her fate.

The Darkness comes to tempt her, calling her, insisting to be let into her head.

'No!' she shouts. 'No, you will not have her! You are the guilty ones!'

In her dreamtime, the air moves and shifts and there it is again, the white dragon shining brightly, moving towards the water's edge breathing out molten hot fire to torch the wriggling creatures.

The Darkness comes in a storming wind expecting to blow the flames back at her, expecting to easily enter her dreaming and control her. Lottie's anger grows as she rises into the air. Feeling Sebastian and Lillian are with her brings her extra strength as she breathes her fire, which grows into a wall of flame in front of the Dark One. Her voice comes whispering fiercely on her fiery breath,

'You will not take her, she is ours.'

The Darkness vanishes out of the dreamtime.

On the slab of rock light begins to come into the girl's open eyes, her lips move, she is saying something. They lean closer,

'I am Willow the singer of songs that lull dragons to sleep, the mouse, the Protector, the glowing light.'

Her voice gets louder as she repeats it over and over. Rhaina falls silent to watch as the young woman sits up looking directly at Lottie. Her mouth opens wide. A long black horned wriggling worm uncurls from inside her. Evil smelling, it screeches out its anger as she vomits it up. Branca doesn't hesitate to cut its head off. It falls, still wriggling to the floor where it gives one final twitch before lying still.

Willow lays back down, her eyes close as she falls asleep, a smile on her tired and wan looking face. Lottie staggers into Branca who holds her up as a voice says,

'What is happening here?'

A tall man in a long cloak has entered the cave led in by Rezto.

'Jack,' cries Lottie.

21: AT LAST
IT BEGINS

In the garden of the Ice Palace with its petrified trees and frozen fountains, a woman sits wrapped in a warm cloak on a low wall. Standing in front of her are her jailers, one of whom is much larger than the other. The two Sylii are typical of their kind, with their round iron hard bodies covered in long dark hair, standing on their many legs that carry them fast over the ground. They have a crab like mouth and four watchful eyes under bushy eyebrows. They can expand themselves upwards to the height of a human being, while their strong pincers also extend to become a lethal weapon. However, the Sylii are not what they seem, certainly not jailers.

The larger one is called Bano Escatara. He is the leader and is speaking to the woman in a voice that is kindly and warm,

'We have more information Princess. Someone else arrived here a short time ago. We couldn't wake you, the drug you were given still works well, but this one,' he flicks a pincer towards his companion, 'was out and about when a fair-haired human arrived so he buried himself to watch. Unfortunately, the human's arrival coincided with that of a group of Shilocks who immediately tried to catch him. The humankind then did an amazing thing. He turned into a large grey wolf to escape, I think with the help of one of the Hobi Rat creatures.'

'Oh, definitely escaped,' giggled his companion Ederoy. 'Oh, most definitely escaped, over the hill and gone.'

Bano Escatara raises his four eyes and wiggles his eyebrows at this most uncalled for intrusion into his report of an important event.

'Jack,' breathes Rhea, 'at last it begins.'

Bano Escatara calls her 'Princess' as a genuine mark of respect. Slim, with beautiful light-coloured hair she has a perfectly shaped face, except there is a scar running down one side of it near her ear. Proof that she is also a fighter. It is in fact the mark of Cravenclaw inflicted many years ago. Her eyes are deep and challenging with feint lines forming at the corners, and of course there is that smile.

'You will see something vastly different soon,' she says to Bano Escatara. 'You will no longer have to play this game of jailer, to protect your kind from these devils that think they have power over you. Even after all the brainwashing and drugs, I have managed with your help to hide away part of my mind. It has enabled me to send occasional messages, albeit not as good as I would wish, but change is coming. Although I cannot speak to them, I have at last managed to send images to my son and daughter.'

'That's a very good thing, but for now we continue to wait, watch and keep up the pretence,' Bano Escatara says.

'Yes,' agrees Rhea. 'We must wait and see what transpires. I wish I knew where Ambrose was imprisoned. He must surely still be alive.'

She looks up at the heavens as the Winter Planet's evening lightshow begins and where, travelling through space, memories of a past time she will recognise seek her out. Enfolded in white light it is a long way off, yet it is coming, only she will know it. The mind that drives it is strong but at present it causes the sender great pain.

22: HARLEQUIN CONFLICTED

In the early morning following Willow's release, at about the time of Rhea's conversation with Bano Escatara, Harlequin is tracking and watching four lesser Metalions. Taking great care not to be seen, he spies on the quartet who are out hunting for a human or two, disobeying strict orders given by Magda Cross. They are in the forest of pine trees that covers a part of the mountain above Christine's farm. Although allies, he won't be able to persuade them to stop, they hate him and he certainly reserves judgement on their usefulness. Magda Cross will be furious with him at this disobedience as she and Cravenclaw are away on the Winter Planet plotting with the others. He is supposed to be keeping an eye on things.

Harlequin is human, a solitary soul damaged in the ferment that brought Horizon to its current position. Twenty years ago, when he was younger the Darkness changed his life rescuing him from a tribe of Owlmen. These cruel fast moving two-legged creatures, covered in feathers and with a deadly bite, captured him when he was very young in some long-forgotten raid. Last year one of their leaders Nosarata was felled by a great blow from Rodrigo when the Owlman looked likely to kill Sergio. They have not been seen on Earth since that time.

He grew up a slave to the Owlmen, a wretched existence being mocked and treated badly all the time. Later he found he could change to a Harlequin although he kept it hidden. The Darkness came upon him walking with the tribe. Recognising his superior intellect, it took him from his miserable life to coach him as a follower.

His fame soon began to spread amongst many of the disciples of evil as a mysterious loner, an architect of various wicked ventures and one who easily passes among humankind. He was someone who stood apart, watching calmly as whatever he had planned came to fruition. Provoked he becomes an extremely dangerous being, changing to the strange looking Harlequin making knives fly from his hand with deadly accuracy.

Spellman is out on the mountain too, having decided to walk the sheep with Christine and Sergio to escape his thoughts and worries about Willow. There has been no news yet on the outcome of the attempt to rescue her. As he looks around, the clear mountain air, the wide expansive landscape and the spring sunshine begin to lift his spirits a little.

Stopping to let the animals graze, they are laughing and chatting about some of Spellman's early and not always successful adventures. Christine is standing a little apart from the other two carrying her sword in a long thin bag across her shoulders. Leaning on a shepherd's crook her loud and infectious laughter echoes down the mountainside. Her face is vibrant, her long auburn hair burnished by the sunlight.

For a moment the shepherdess looks back at the trees, the watcher hiding there is suddenly lost and confused by an emotion he has never felt before. A feeling that when it comes is often instant, beyond logic, takes no prisoners and Harlequin is struck hard by it.

Deep in the pine forest the Metalions have heard them, their prowling gait quickens at the sound of the sheep and the laughter; the scent of humans is strong in their nostrils. The four metal creatures slow to an ungainly walk creeping towards the edge of the forest to watch. They are breathing heavily both from excitement and exertion. They don't have a great deal of stamina and have prowled around for most of the night.

Harlequin doesn't move. Confused by this new feeling which is reeling around in his head clouding his reason, he hesitates. Should he attack the three shepherds with the Metalions, after all they are his enemy? Perhaps better to wait for an outcome that he can report back to Magda Cross. Suddenly his hesitation doesn't matter.

The four Metalions recover their breath and immediately attack, breaking out of the woodland and fanning out as they charge. Four monsters with swords and axes in hand scattering the sheep in all directions. The two dogs rush at the creatures barking but are easily batted aside.

Spellman is fast as always. The air moves and the Metalions face a very tall black man in an armoured suit like a new skin, who rushes at them with a glittering sword in his hand. He is followed by Sergio drawing his long knife. Spellman ducks and dodges past the fastest of them who is nowhere near quick enough, as the Dragon Sword slashes sideways cutting through the metal and both its calf muscles and down it goes. The warrior quickly dispatches it before rushing on to engage another of the Metal ones. Sergio meantime has caught one of them off guard watching Spellman. The Metalion finds itself hit broadside by this giant of a man and over they both go.

Christine has managed to get her newly acquired sword out of its long sheath as the fourth Metalion comes for her. She manages to parry several blows from its axe and sword, but she is too slow and her sword is soon spinning into the air making her defenceless. The creature takes a very quick look around to see its companions are not doing well. Grunting, it grabs Christine by the hair, hoists her over its shoulders and makes for the trees. Crashing into the wood with Christine kicking and screaming it blunders past the hidden Harlequin who follows it moving swiftly and silently.

The Metalion manages to get some distance into the wood before running out of breath. It throws its captive down by a tree knocking the air out of her, making her dizzy. Raising its axe, beginning to drool at the mouth, the metal being makes a low guttural noise at the thought of a kill. Then it hears a sharp noise from behind and turns to look. There is a whizzing sound and a 'plop,' as the knife slices through into its left eye and on into its brain, dropping the monster to the ground in an instant.

Minutes later Christine gets up shakily as Spellman and Sergio arrive. Sergio, who is covered in blood from a wound on his head sees the Metal One lying dead with the knife still sticking out of its eye.

'Are you ok?' He asks.

'Who did this?' asks Spellman.

'Yes, to the first and haven't a clue to the second,' Christine says.

'What, no idea at all?'

'None, except I caught a glimpse of something

red and black,' she says.

'Mm,' says Spellman looking around. 'Let's get back to the sheep.'

Christine starts to move off followed by the others, warily watching the wood for any more of the enemy that might be hiding there.

The sheep have circled back to where one of the dogs is sitting looking down at the other lying still on the ground.

Harlequin now several kilometres away stops to listen; there is nothing coming after him. The trees sway in a light breeze, somehow bringing a frisson of loneliness that he shakes off and then carries on wondering to himself why he is smiling.

23: ALL TOGETHER NOW

Willow, still sleeping, has been left to rest and recover under the care of Agnes and Eda's wife Rhaina while the others return to Christine's farm. Meg and Tess lying against the warm wall of the house, watch them sitting around the table in the sun talking together. Meg has a large wound on her head from the Metalion's blow which has been expertly dressed and attended to by Christine.

It is a coming together filled with mixed emotions for Jack. Hearing the shocking news about Willow's part in the death of Sebastian and Lillian is making him unusually quiet, forgetting everything else. Lottie is worried and keeps looking at him surreptitiously noticing that he has changed. His whole manner when he does speak is more mature and assertive, he even seems to have grown a little larger and now has a beard.

Sergio has recounted their fight with the Metalions.

'We still can't find out who it was that helped Christine by killing the Metalion. Whoever it was had great knife throwing skills.'

'I wish I had been able to see more so at least I could thank my rescuer. However, it is obvious I need more training with the sword,' Christine says looking at Branca.

Spellman has conflicting emotions too. He is happy to hear of Willow's recovery yet angry at what she has been through and ready for revenge. Sadness also grips him as he is very aware that Jack and Lottie will also be feeling angry and unsure about Willow. He shakes himself out of his stupor to speak to Jack,

'So, you have acquired a new skill which is no ordinary achievement brother. It's a relief to see you back with us again, perhaps you should tell us what happened to you?'

Rodrigo surveys the group his eyes growing flint hard, knowing they must all move on from grieving for Sebastian and Lillian. Their enemies will not stop trying to catch them. He also says quietly to Jack,

'Yes, that's a good idea, we need to press on. Magda Cross will not take the demise of the four Metalions lightly or Willow's release when she finds out.'

Jack's head comes up, for a moment the light dances in his eyes as he gives a broad grin, shaking himself up mentally to say,

'It is a fantastic story, wait until you hear about a Wind Horse called Persephone. Although the most important news is,' he pauses to look at Lottie, 'I have found our Mother, or at least I know where she is. I have found Rhea.'

This brings spontaneous applause and a burst of questions.

Lottie is stunned. Rodrigo raises his hand to calm everyone with,

'Have you seen her Jack?'

'No, but I know some very brave and interesting furry creatures who have and what's more they knew I was coming!'

He rattles on to tell them of his adventure on the Winter Planet, about Lennie the Hobi and the meeting of the wicked ones. He tells them of the Ice Dragon Smorkis with her many servants, the strange Shilock creatures, and although he has not seen them, of his mother's jailers the even stranger Sylii. He reserves until last the meeting with the Magician Chingis and the Wind Horses.

'Wait,' says Rodrigo, 'did you say Chingis?'

'Yes,' said Jack, 'he is a particularly good friend to us. Do you know him?'

'Oh yes, he has become a legend. We knew him as Chingis the Mongol because he came from a population that looked vaguely like a race of earthbound people of that name. They fought hard against the evil Interventionists. He is a strong brave warrior who had a partner, a black-haired lady called Moon; the rumour is they lost each other somehow. He went his own way some-time after the loss of Ambrose and Rhea.'

Jack shrugs and continues,

'I don't really know much about his history. He is known by many on the Winter Planet as 'the Hermit', a mysterious man held in some awe who has developed extraordinary powers. He helped us to escape from spying on Magda Cross and her cronies and that towering hooded figure. He had called up the two Wind Horses, a black stallion and Persephone, and we were carried to a land of hot geysers and a great warm lake. We met the other two Hobis Hannibal and Caramel there. They had been searching for someone to tell about the captured and imprisoned woman they had seen. They described her exactly as she appears in the visions we have been having.'

He looks again at his sister. Lottie's smile echoes her mother's, her eyes shine while Jack carries on,

'Lottie, with your special visionary skills beginning to develop you should really talk to Chingis. He has a profound real magic that can control the elements.'

Christine asks,

'Does the black stallion have a name?'

'He is called Gaanbater and he is his own master,' comes the reply from the one who strides out of the sunlight towards them.

'I am sorry I'm late Jack but we had one or two things to sort out before I left the Winter Planet.'

'Chingis!' shouts Jack jumping up. 'You came. Welcome!'

'Indeed, I have and there is someone else I managed to bring with me.'

With that, a black and white furry creature standing as tall as possible steps out from behind the Magician to look warily around saying,

'You got proper warm sunshine here. I am going to have to change my coat if this continues!'

'Lennie!' laughs Jack, 'you are very welcome here too.'

Rodrigo gets up and walks towards Chingis his arms spread wide saying,

'Welcome back to the war Brother.'

They hug each other and are joined by Branca and Spellman. Jack surveys the group and says quietly to himself,

'Mother, we are coming for you.'

In a valley not so far away Magda Cross is back and in human form; she burns with an ice cold fury as she hears from Harlequin about the events with the Metalions. Dynasta, who has nothing but contempt for this tall good-looking man is having to back away from any idea that their actions were justified.

'There are many of us. I will bring more here now,' he says. 'We will simply overrun them and destroy them all.'

'Just like that,' Magda Cross says angrily rounding on him. 'You are forgetting Ironjaw with his daughters, and they won't be the only creatures that rally to their cause. That is not the fight we want here and now. We need to weaken them bit by bit,' she points a finger at Dynasta. 'You will not do anything until I say so. You have no idea the power you are facing if you disobey my instructions. Our Master wants those twins.'

Dynasta growls acceptance, as Naptha the Demon diverts her attention by pointing out they still have a spy in the camp.

'Yes, we will need her to keep us informed.'

'I saw her a little while ago. They have lost the boy twin. Upset with the death of his parents he has disappeared.'

'Find him, find him. If he is still missing the next time you speak to Willow I will bring more help. We need them to be destroyed here on this planet.'

At the Farmhouse it is dark, plans are being laid, a great feast has been prepared and is being consumed. Ironjaw and Synabeth are there. His other daughter Gretchen watches from high on the mountain, and Bonny the eagle is a kilometre away at the beginning of the track high in a tree also watching. The serious and intense discussions are interspersed with laughter as anecdotes and memories are dragged up.

Lottie walks away from the group as the moon comes into the sky to sit quietly on her own. Ironjaw turns to look at her and shuffles towards her.

'It is good to see you again Sister but you seem worried.'

Lottie looks gratefully up at the Dragon.

'Oh, and it is good to see you my friend. It's Willow that's on my mind. I know she wasn't the person we know when she became directly involved in the death of Lillian and Sebastian. It's just that I can't come to terms with their loss and I miss them dreadfully. It will be hard to be with her.'

'I can help you with a little healing dragon breath perhaps?' the Red Dragon murmurs.

'No,' says Jack approaching them and overhearing the discussion, 'I have thought about this. We should not mask the pain, instead we should try and turn it against those that are really the guilty ones. I don't know how I will feel either with Willow, but we are on the same side and she has always been our greatest friend.'

'Well said,' Ironjaw replies.

Lottie hugs her brother,

'And of course, that is exactly how Sebastian and Lillian would see it,' she says, as tears prick the corners of her eyes.

Down at the entrance to the track, the rider and the dog have appeared again silhouetted in the moonlight. Gretchen spots them and simply glides off her ledge to show herself. The demon's blue eyes trace her flight to land somewhere under the trees. Naptha shrugs his shoulders and heeds the warning, tonight is obviously not the time to try and meet with Willow, so he turns the great horse away.

Everyone is getting sleepy and the conversations are slowing down.

Rodrigo says quietly to Chingis the Magician,

'Are you really alone?'

The Magician's eyes look up to scan the starry heavens,

'I searched and searched. I never found her,' he says quite simply shaking his head.

This brings a pause in the conversation into which Lennie throws himself,

'Oh, but you should see this one riding with Gaanbater, it is utterly awesome.'

They all smile, and Jack says,

'Talking of which how did the Wind Horses get there?'

Chingis looks up, his eyes for a moment fix on Jack and he says enigmatically,

'They come out of past times, of ancient whispers that have been forgotten yet wait to be heard again, out of words said in the right way and out of believing. Persephone is waiting for you Jack although you will have to learn to call her for yourself.'

The next day Rodrigo meets with Darius, dragon fighter and Councillor, one side of his face livid red from the fire of the Ice-Dragon. Part of the plan is to inform him, now the new Deputy Leader of the Council, what is happening on the Winter Planet. Darius has been questioning Rodrigo closely and has grown silent, his eyes focussed somewhere in the distance. Eventually he says,

'This is all good news Rodrigo but how do we break it to the inhabitants of Horizon? These are uncertain times. I am being asked to stand against Adeth for the leadership of the Council, and to strengthen the Protectors still further to become even more proactive in defending ourselves.'

The revered war hero answers his own question,

'Yesterday, I addressed a packed meeting on doing just that and increasing the powers of some Protectors. It was an edgy meeting because after

I explained how precarious the situation was becoming, citizens became alarmed worrying about us losing control. We are getting close to our society breaking down. All of us want the days of safety and stability back free from fear and suspicion. Finding and rescuing Rhea, with the possibility of Ambrose being alive would be a big boost to morale, but it needs to be a fact not a rumour. I suggest we operate quickly and secretly to rescue her, making sure she is safe with us before saying anything. Will you lead that mission?'

'Of course, I will,' Rodrigo replies, it is the only part of the conversation that has made complete sense to him.

Darius claps him on the shoulder,

'Excellent! You will be doing me personally a great favour. I still miss them both. Ambrose saved my life, gave me a new one and we need his wisdom. I was lucky that he shared a little of it with me.'

Rodrigo says, 'We had thought we would make it short and sharp. Go in quickly, get Rhea out and safely away without starting a major incident. That fight may come later.'

Darius agrees,

'I think that is absolutely what's required. Please keep me informed of progress and be careful of Smorkis.'

Later, Rodrigo wonders to himself why he had not spoken about Chingis. Perhaps it was because just for a few seconds the image of the huge tree in the desert came to him, almost a warning to be careful. Darius is now openly seeking power to lead the Galaxy in a way that Rodrigo does not wholly agree with. He cannot however fault the would-be dragon slayer's concerns about the rise of fear and suspicion. He goes to see Adeth who greets him warmly.

24: A CHANGE IN THE TEMPERATURE

Three days later on the Planet of ice and snow the first signs of a thaw are setting in. As the brief summertime approaches, branches on the petrified trees are beginning to drip. Jack on Persephone, her beautiful wings folded back, is riding quietly and slowly up to the doors of the Ice Palace. Getting remarkably close without a challenge, Persephone stops and a puzzled Jack notices the great doors are ajar. He feels no sense of danger.

The original plan was to simply walk up to the doors and ask to speak to Rhea his mother and see what transpired. From left and right come two running figures, Branca and Spellman who disappear one after the other into the Winter Palace. Jack is joined by Chingis on the back of the magnificent black stallion Gaanbater, the javelin with its sharp prism rotating slowly with alternating distinct colours.

'There appears to be no one here,' Jack says.

'So, it would seem.'

It is noticeably quiet, not a sound disturbs the air. The sun is reflecting off the cliff tops as they both look around the empty landscape. Very soon the two Protectors return from searching the Palace.

"There isn't anyone in there as far as we can see, just empty corridors and hollow rooms,' reports Spellman. 'Rhea is gone.'

Jack's face briefly shows his disappointment at the anti-climax of not meeting his mother, but he recovers to ask the question,

'Where have they taken her and where are the Syllii that you said lived here Chingis?'

'Perhaps they can answer that?'

The Magician points to an area of snow to their left where something is coming out of the ground like a corkscrew out of a bottle, followed by another and then another. Soon there are many of them, but one is much bigger than the rest. Surrounded, the four of them Spellman, Chingis, Branca and Jack look in amazement and some amusement at these round hairy creatures with many legs spinning out of the snow. They are even more amazed as some of the Sylli decide to raise themselves to full height and uncurl their decidedly wicked looking pincers.

Chingis slides from Gaanbater's back with Jack following suit, and they walk towards the tallest Syllus.

'I think you must be the famous Bano Escatara,' says Chingis in a voice full of respect. 'We are very pleased to meet you.'

'Oh, he's heard of you,' twitters Ederoy.

'Ah,' says Bano Escatara his four eyes twinkling, 'he is just trying to butter us up. You are the Hermit no doubt, and you,' pointing a large pincer at Jack, 'are Jack, Rhea's son and these two are Protectors. Although what good they have done us around here I don't know. Where is Lottie and Rodrigo? It looks like you have also forgotten to bring some dragons. However, we are pleased to meet you.'

'How do you know so much about us?' Jack asks.

'From the Princess. We had no choice but to keep her hidden with us as we cannot resist the combined forces of that Chimera, the two dragons and their army of sycophantic servants the Shilocks. There are also the visits of the humanoid in the cloak they call their Lord, and of course the Darkness is ever present.

'We have with the Princess as our prisoner, played a waiting game. They did not manage to completely eradicate her memory or some of her abilities, but they don't know that. Although the drug she was given makes her very tired from time to time, she is strong. When you turned up Jack, we were expecting the tide to turn against the wicked ones.'

'And it will,' says Jack grimly,' but where is my mother now?'

'I don't know. They came, took her away, telling us to leave the Ice Palace for a while so that it would look deserted. They have in the past been moving her around the Galaxy but I have a feeling she is still here.'

'Ahem,' comes a voice from outside the circle, where three furry creatures have quietly stolen up on them all. 'I think we might have some information,' Hannibal says as the Sylli stand aside to let them through.

They all look at the Hobis.

'Our friends and relations have sent messages to tell us that the unnecessary ones are still here, coming and going in the Ice Valley, which may well mean Rhea is here as well.'

Lennie looks warily around but everyone seems to be relaxed.

Chingis says,

'Then we will find out. We will ride to the mountain where Lennie and Jack stayed when they came to find me. We will be able to see from there what transpires. Will you join us?' he asks

Bano Escatara.

'Yes,' comes the reply. 'We can move quickly but even so we will be half a day behind you.'

Branca and Spellman wonder how they were going to get there, and again wishing it were possible to transport themselves over short distances, when there is a call. A high-pitched neighing that comes from Gaanbater followed by a gentle whinnying. They hear an answering neigh like an echo and two Wind Horses, the so-called Ice Maidens, descend looking magnificent with wings outspread and gleaming in the sunlight.

Lennie opens his mouth to ask the question, but before any words come out Chingis lifts him up on Gaanbater, while Jack helps Caramel onto Persephone and Hannibal gets to ride with Branca. They all mount up and Chingis says,

'We will look for you tomorrow.'

'It will be near sunrise,' replies Bano Escatara.

The riders and horses climb into the heavens and are soon dots on the horizon.

25: SHUSH!

It is now twilight in the Ice Valley, the darkening sky is beginning to come alive with the auroral lights arcing across it. The two-headed chimera Magda Cross is again in this place with the Dragons Cravenclaw and Smorkis. Her lioness head speaks directly to them as the serpent one moves around watching the landscape,

'They will think she is here, that creature Bano Escatara will tell them. The male twin will come. He will not be able to resist trying to find his mother and we will have him.'

The Dragons are silent, so she repeats,

'Be sure, he will come.'

Cravenclaw, the black fearless and loyal dragon regards his evil mistress. He loves her two heads, the long body and the stinging tail. Her wings are folded back as she stands looking at them on long clawed feet. He is in awe of her ability to hide in human form. They are as one in their hatred of the creatures of the light, and they embrace the Darkness as it rushes across the white plain to envelop the three of them.

'This time we will have them all,' Cravenclaw says as his massive head goes back and he emits a huge roar, followed by a jet of fire that shoots up into the night sky.

On the opposite side, Jack looks out across the white expanse into the Ice Valley and sees the fire jet. He is some way from the cave that he stayed in before, sitting on a large rock with Chingis and the inevitable Lennie.

'We need to be sure that my Mother is over there,' he says. 'We can't just attack the place; it would be a complete waste of our resources if she is hidden somewhere else. Some of us may not come back and we will have lost lives for nothing.'

'You are planning a foray into the enemy's camp?' asks Chingis. 'They will be waiting for you I suspect. There is something odd about the fact that they moved Rhea just before we turned up. It seems too much of a coincidence. We kept our secrets close. I felt sure Magda Cross knew nothing of our activities here or about your earlier visit to this planet.'

'Yes, I have been thinking that they knew we were coming as well,' Jack agrees. 'It is frustrating not to know who or what we are up against, and they could easily move her again.'

'Look at those reflections from the moon out there in the middle of the plain.' Chingis points to where there appears to be a narrow ribbon of wavering light. 'It is getting warmer and the river is starting to form. It will become a raging torrent as the ice and snow melts, soon the land will be green and verdant for a short while.'

'I have to go across there now. It is the only way of finding out if they are keeping her prisoner in that valley,' Jack says. 'If she will let me, I plan to ride on Persephone to get dropped off as near as possible and then creep into spy on them.'

'I can raise a mist for a short time to provide you with cover, but we need to tell the others.' Chingis replies.

When they return to the cave entrance, they find that Ironjaw the Red Dragon and his two daughters Gretchen and Synabeth have arrived. Jack tells them the plan. At once Spellman offers to go with him but Branca shakes her head to say,

'You are not a Wolf and you will be quickly spotted. Jack you are going to have to be incredibly careful. Chingis is right, they may well be waiting for you to do just this.'

Jack shrugs, 'At this moment I can't see any other option that will give us the information. If Synabeth or Gretchen fly in they will be easily spotted.'

Lennie pipes up,

'I will come with you.'

Jack starts to shake his head but the Hobi goes on to say,

'I will also not be so easily seen and you may need to send a messenger back.'

Jack makes the decision,

'Thank you. We have done it before and I can't think of a better companion. We must go now.'

He closes his eyes and lets his mind travel to a sunlit green valley where there are several Wind Horses grazing in a field. One looks up when he calls her name. A short time later Persephone arrives. The others watch Jack holding onto her mane with Lennie sat on his lap as she flaps her strong wings, and the three of them are on their way into the night.

Chingis smiles to himself seeing Jack's expertise at calling the Wind Horse, before turning to the group saying,

'Right. We need a battle plan for an attack or a rescue if it all goes wrong. Before that though a little mist.'

Moving away from them, holding the javelin in the air he starts to quietly repeat an indecipherable chant. As the prism speeds up he points it across the plain at the distant valley.

Jack and Lennie see the mist forming as they look down on the stream that will soon become a river; it curves across the plain before it disappears underground. Even at their height the air is getting warmer. As the mist grows dense, the Wind Horse glides into land softly near the entrance to the valley and the pair slip from her back. Jack looks up at Persephone and goes into the dreamtime where she is standing looking at him. He says,

'Thank you, my friend, will you wait for us?'

The Wind Horse bows her head.

The air moves and the Great Grey Wolf appears beside Lennie. They start to move cautiously forward. Nothing appears to be moving in the mist, so they shift a bit quicker until they find some rocks scattered at the beginning of the valley. Beginning to creep forward from one icy rock to another, taking it in turns to lead, they climb higher. Still nothing seems to be moving, all the shapes that appear out of the mist seem to be static.

'So far so good,' whispers Jack, 'but the mist must lift soon and I feel a sense of great danger near us.'

Lennie grins and whispers back,

'I don't think you have to be a wolf to feel that.'

They climb a little further to find a place to settle down as the mist begins to thin and then lift. As it does, shapes below them begin to take on a reality as they look downwards. Looking up directly at them is a small army of Shilocks, their hollow eyes shining like torches in the night. Jack starts to say something when a great weight hits his head and he slumps to the ground unconscious. Lennie moves like quicksilver, dodging between the rocks as Smorkis shoots a gout of fire at him.

'Don't bother with that one,' comes a voice from a little way off. 'We have what we want. They will soon know that, which is perfect for us as they will try to rescue him and we will have them all.'

Magda Cross looks at the Great Grey Wolf lying beneath her. Her serpent head sweeping down to look closely at the prone figure.

'When he wakes, we will bind him and put him with his mother. A pity they won't be able to talk to each other,' she laughs as she changes back.

Lennie runs and runs to get to the stream which is now much wider, growing deep and very cold. He comes to a stop as he spots the Wind Horse waiting patiently, and beside her is one of the prettiest, yet startlingly awesome beings he has ever seen.

Back in the Ice Valley Magda Cross is bating Jack, who on waking, although groggy has transformed back. She is thoroughly enjoying herself.

'My dear boy, I am so pleased to see you are recovering from the unfortunate knock on your head. We did need to ensure you stayed with us especially as you were so kind as to do exactly as we expected. After all this nonsense that has been going on we seem to have found you are not terribly clever.'

Magda Cross is looking her best in human form, sophisticated and charming, enjoying Jack's discomfort at being caught. The blow to his head is aching badly, his eyes appear unfocused and he drifts in and out of consciousness. Her triumphant and mocking tone is having negligible effect on him.

'Never mind, we shall enjoy your company much more when we have some of the others too.'

Her charm mask slips, her eyes glow red and that long tongue slips out as she waves at a group of Shilocks to carry him away.

Returning to consciousness a little later Jack wakes with a groan as his eyes slowly open to look around. There are several fire torches in brackets on the wall of the cave, the light from which picks out the woman lying curled up asleep in one of the corners. Jack attempts to move but finds he is bound tightly with thick rope.

'Mother,' he calls to her several times, hoping to wake her but without success. She lies still breathing slowly and deeply.

It is now the early hours of the morning and very dark. Across the other side of the plain, Chingis is talking to Rodrigo who arrived to join them earlier.

'Although I fear the worst has happened, perhaps we should wait until dawn's light before doing anything.'

'I agree,' says Rodrigo, 'then we shall create a storm that they will not expect. The Chimera knows we are here, however, they don't know how many of us there are or who is with us.'

'That's true,' agrees Chingis.

That night many lie awake watching the stars, they know that in the morning all may change.

A benevolent eye is also straining to watch, locked away and tortured by imprisonment and inactivity, yet still able to summon the strength to get the occasional glimpse of events as they unfold.

Ambrose concentrates deeply but the messages will not leave his mind and reach across the divides of space. He knows what his children will face. He is mentally shackled and torn, his mind shrouded in the void where only the occasional pale images of real time slip through, but he continues to strive for better clarity.

The hours drip by slowly for his son Jack, lying frustrated, as he tries to figure out how deep in the mountain they are and how to escape. Rhea in the corner of the cave sleeps on unaware of the impending fight.

However, outside a small Mouse, a Dormouse is scampering around the rocks at the beginning of the Ice Valley. All over the area there is much activity as more and more Shilocks are turning up. Smorkis is in the middle of them looking resplendent and gleaming in the moonlight.

Further back, the Chimera and Cravenclaw are deep in conversation while the Darkness swirls through them all. The Mouse gains the higher ground undetected and watches. She is brown and white with dark twinkling eyes, very sharp teeth and a long tail ending in a tassel. Willow's blood runs cold as she sees further up the valley, standing beside a large dark hole in the mountainside is Dynasta. His huge bulk is easy to spot, while just below him waiting patiently are at least ten Metalions.

'That's where they are hidden,' the Mouse whispers to herself.

Summoning up her courage, she moves slowly from rock to rock to get past the metal mass that is Dynasta, his breath whistling through rows of teeth. Intent on watching the preparations going on in the valley below, they don't notice the little one that scurries past them into the cave.

Jack is drooping with tiredness, his chin on his chest, until his ultra-sharp hearing brings him a slight scuffling noise. His head snaps back. A small furry creature skids into the room, comes to a halt to raise up on her hind legs, putting a small paw to her mouth to whisper theatrically,

'Shush!'

26: RAIDERS AT FIRST LIGHT

As the dawn arrives the raiders come on fast and furious without hesitation. Knowing they are expected the warriors do not flinch. The task must be done whatever the cost.

There are now hundreds of Shilocks on the plain in front of the valley. Their mistress the Ice Dragon Smorkis stands in their midst rearing up on her hind legs, roaring out as she catches sight of the Wind Horses.

Gaanbater is majestic, snorting loudly, his wings beating the air, hooves flashing, a black statement of muscle and power. On his back, the Magician carrying the javelin in his left-hand stabs light into the Darkness as it tries to weave its way in and out of the Shilocks. The shafts of intense laser light spread out as they hit the shadow which quivers as though in pain. Eventually it disappears to hover at the edge of the battle.

Expertly gripping the galloping stallion with

his knees, Chingis unsheathes the curved sword from his back with his other hand. Leaning over he swings the blade to skittle down as many of the Shilocks as he can. The other three Wind Horses carrying Spellman, Branca and Rodrigo fly past him heading for the valley entrance.

At the edges of the army of Shilocks, strange round and hairy creatures are springing up out of the snow, their many legs spinning them around catching the ghost like beings off guard. The Sylii and the Hobi Rats attack by jumping in twos and threes on to the pale creatures doing deadly work with pincers or biting furiously. It is a hard fight, their adversaries have very tough skin and are strong, able to use their talons and teeth to good effect.

Smorkis takes to the air raging, spitting fire only to be met by Ironjaw. The Red Dragon and the Iced One crash into each other high in the air, teeth, claw and fire rage above the battlefield. Gretchen and Synabeth fly around them to head up the valley to join the three Protectors who are engaging a wave of Metalions behind which are Cravenclaw, Dynasta and the Chimera Magda Cross. Although it was expected, the attack has caught them by surprise in its intensity and timing, but these evil ones are ready for the fight.

Branca and Spellman act together jumping off the Wind Horses and almost like ballet dancers, they whirl and spin, chopping the Metalions down, but there are many now. Behind them comes the transformed Rodrigo. The Grizzly Bear roars; standing three metres tall he powers into the metal monsters knocking them aside felling some with a single blow.

In the cave all is quiet as Willow changes back to untie the ropes. Eventually they come loose so Jack shakes himself free getting stiffly to his feet. Willow begins to glow softly, a low peaceful light as she approaches Rhea who has not moved. The lovely one bends down to look at her and gently shakes her shoulder. Jack looks at them both momentarily awestruck, this is the Willow he knows and has badly missed. She turns to look up at him as they both struggle for the right words to say to each other before she whispers softly,

'There is a deep magic here, we have to wake your mother up and get you both out.'

A sadness is in her eyes as she looks at him. 'No one knows I followed you. I am going outside to see what is happening and how many guards there are now.'

Jack manages a smile, nods his head as the air moves and the mouse scurries out of sight. Jack walks over to Rhea, the mother he has never seen or heard, and looking down on her serene face whispers,

'Where are you now mother?'

The raging begins to rise in him again, the injustice done to Rhea and Ambrose, the death of his earth parents, the capture of Willow, the sheer evil of the devils and demons that drive his enemies infuses his very core with a white heat.

Willow returns to say there is one guard left outside.

The Metalion is watching the fighting when there is a noise behind it. Turning around it sees a girl that glows softly, even in the daylight shadows, but it has no time for appreciation. The Wolf comes bounding out at it snarling, all his anger bound into a leap that catches the Metalion by surprise and sends it backwards, sliding and slipping on the melting ice and snow to disappear into the valley below. Managing to skid to a stop, the Great Grey Wolf's howl echoes loudly across the battle and all know he is free.

Willow and the Wolf look at each other for a few moments before Jack changes back. Desperate to speak to her he hesitates, in a heartbeat she raises her hand palm outwards, the air shifts and she is gone. Jack shakes his head and sighs, then turns to race down the mountain to join the fight. Above him, the two huge dragons dominate the sky as they crash into each other repeatedly their fiery battle loud and awesome.

Smorkis suddenly misses her attack and immediately Ironjaw is on her back his teeth buried in her neck. They roll over and over in the air until they crash to the ground scattering the Shilocks. The Red Dragon is on top and rolls off his opponent to be first to his feet ready to fight on. There is no movement from Smorkis. She is unconscious, her eyes are closed, her breathing shallow. Ironjaw is about to finish her off when a squadron of Shilocks attack, biting and clawing at him, some managing to jump on his back.

Shrugging them off, he turns away from Smorkis to help Chingis fight the still strong army of pale ghosts. It is not long before it becomes obvious they are being defeated. Many are dead or are creeping away wounded as the sun climbs into the sky brightening the day. Soon Ironjaw and the Magician can join the other three Protectors, leaving the Sylii and the Hobi Rats to despatch or chase off the remaining Shilocks. Meanwhile Gretchen and Synabeth are attacking Cravenclaw like angry bees, keeping him occupied as they duck and dive, in and out, around and around.

Eventually, a line begins to form across the sunlit snow-covered landscape. The ferocious Grizzly Bear is joined by Spellman and Branca, then by Chingis on Gaanbater still snarling and snorting. Ironjaw joins the line calling his daughters to his side and the Great Grey Wolf bounds down to join them. They all advance towards their enemies.

There are now just the three of the enemy left with the remnants of Shilocks and Metalions. However, they are powerful, full of hate and more than ready to fight on. The Chimera Magda Cross's heads roar and spit fire, Cravenclaw is up on his back legs, even bigger than Ironjaw who he longs to kill, while Dynasta with his implacable hatred of human beings is ready to slaughter all of them if he can.

The Darkness hurries across the ground that is melting fast to join the fight, trying to come between the two sides as it has done before. Chingis shoots bolts of light into it, however it has little effect this time as they pass straight through. The Dark Power spirals up in front of the three evil ones to shield them.

They take no heed of its dark folds; they are raging, gone beyond sanity and just want to kill those that face them. The formless entity becomes intense, pitch black and focused as it swirls around forming a high column out of which emerges the black cloaked humanoid.

He will not risk losing his outnumbered dark followers who are so eager to do his bidding. His hood hangs over whatever it is he has for a face. The air moves, going out of focus as the creature transmutes growing taller, then as the Darkness swirls around him it happens again so that he grows even larger. The day grows dim as the humanoid commands the landscape and for a moment everything stops to listen.

As he looks down on them a noise is heard from

inside the shadow of the hood. Low at first, it becomes a symphony of hissing and sighing sounds, followed by a cacophony of eerie fast repeated and discordant notes. Like a hammer banging on an anvil as cymbals clash, it echoes out across the plain. The noise begins to beat out a rhythm crashing around them, it rises to a shriek as a hot wind comes, a thunderous vortex issuing out of the hood smelling of putrid meat. It carries the stink of history and death. The company are transfixed unable to move.

'We have raised their devil!' Chingis shouts, trying to be heard above the noise, 'we must attack it.'

Trying to move forward, they struggle against the hurricane of loathing, then suddenly the wind and the noise stop. A searing hot silence follows. A voice strident and clear comes to them,

'I bring powers that were lost in the unimaginable time past. I am time present and time future and I come to claim you. I am you and your dreams. You cannot escape me; inside yourself I am there, the dark that follows light. Look at me, look at me, I will become the face you will see when you look in your mirror. You are finished.'

The humanoid-like creature lowers its dark hood towards them and they all begin to feel the pull of a terrible weariness, a great desire to sleep.

Gaanbater unaffected by all of this rears up,

his hooves flashing, shaking the Magician awake who points the javelin, the prism whirling to fire several shafts of burning light into the dark hood. For a moment it looks as though nothing has happened, then the hooded creature raises its arms to the sky. The air shimmers and shakes, all seems unfocused, then all the wicked ones are gone, disappeared into the air as the light of day returns.

The companions, the Dragons, the Bear, the Wolf, the Protectors and the Magician all look around them. The thaw continues. Trees are already beginning to bud; a small yellow bird flies onto a branch to puff out its chest before singing out its song of renewal.

'Light follows dark,' Chingis says, and they all smile.

Jack asks,

'What, who, was that?'

Chingis replies,

'He is our worst nightmares, our worst fears, almost the embodiment of the Darkness. He is often called Typhon, but he really has no name. I saw him once many years ago dressed exactly like that. His power seems to have grown immensely and I don't remember that disgusting smell. He comes to protect his children, his disciples, which does mean we have made an impression. We must find where he hides and soon.'

'Look,' interrupts Rodrigo pointing to Smorkis who has risen shakily to her feet.

They all turn to look and see next to her is another dragon, smaller, slimmer and perfectly white sharply defined against the grey Ice Dragon. They move warily towards the two of them. The White Dragon regards them with deep set eyes that shine out with intelligence and mystery bowing her head slightly. Chingis the magician his face beaming with a big smile raises his javelin.

'Lottie,' Ironjaw says. 'At last you are come to your calling.'

Jack, who has kept Lottie's secret about her alter self shifts back and says, grinning,

'Sister did you have to be so perfectly formed? I am completely eclipsed.'

The White Dragon looks up at Ironjaw and says,

'We need you to make your peace with this one. Smorkis has been badly used and duped. She has lost her children and the wicked ones have left her behind but they will not leave her alive here. They will come back for her. She must fly north to where the ice never melts to recharge herself. At some point my friend you need to hear her story.'

Ironjaw looks straight at Smorkis for a few moments until a signal, a small gleam of light ancient and timeless passes between them. He says,

'So be it. I will fly with her just in case there is

trouble.'

Lottie shapeshifts back and says,

'That is generous my friend, thank you,' she turns to Jack to ask.

'And where is our Mother?'

27: THE LADY OF THE DOG SOLDIERS

Before they move off Ironjaw asks Smorkis to tell him her story. The Ice Dragon is still slightly dazed, bleeding from various wounds, her energy trickling away helped on by the warmth of the thaw. She tells him quickly how she has been tricked, deceived by the Darkness and Cravenclaw into believing that it was the Protectors and their leaders who stole or killed her son and daughter.

The Red Dragon begins to understand the weight of sorrow and rage this She-Dragon carries.

'I think there is someone you should meet,' Smorkis says. 'We should not fly to the far North but transport to one of this planet's moons.'

Ironjaw looks at her for a moment then nods his great head.

The moon when they arrive is bitterly cold which invigorates Smorkis. The two dragons are on top of a mountain from which they look down on a landscape full of craters and long valleys. The mountains around them seem to be uninhabited with steep ascents full of ice and snow, a light astral wind blows constantly. Apart from the wind there is silence, dragon breath punctures the air. It is a wild and barren place where the pale sun which is beginning to set is not warm enough to melt the ice.

Smorkis tells Ironjaw she has been here before,

'It was the first place I looked for my children. It didn't take long for me to realise they were not here. However, I did meet someone else who I am sure will find us soon.'

Ironjaw turns his head and looks at her,

'Who do you mean?'

'Be patient, they will come and introduce themselves.'

As the night comes on, they both hear a low guttural bark followed by an answering call which echoes across the empty landscape.

'So, you have come again my friend. Why are you in the company of one of our enemies?' A gruff low voice cuts through the silence like a knife.

Ironjaw wheels his great body around to find he is facing a rare sight, a Snarkle, one of the largest dog soldiers he has ever seen. She is standing upright, her completely white fur standing out against the dimming sky although against the snow and ice she is almost invisible. Her eyes are sharp and wary, he notices she has one bright blue eye and one green; her tail is flicking in irritation and the sharp spines along her back are standing erect.

Smorkis reacts quickly,

'He is not the enemy. We have been duped, our trust betrayed, the Black Dragon lied to us.'

A small gout of fire issued from the Snarkle,

'Tell me,' she says, completely unafraid by the presence of the two magnificent and dangerous creatures standing before her, the Red One with fire licking the edges of his mouth. Smorkis turns her head to Ironjaw,

'Let me introduce you to Skadi. She is the Lady of the Dog Soldiers, the leader of these ancient ones. Skadi, this dragon Ironjaw is to be trusted.'

'We may be ancient but we are a lot less now,' interjects Skadi. 'If you speak for him, we will move somewhere more sheltered and you can tell me your story.'

It is then, as they begin to move with the nightly aurora lights rising to brighten the snowy wastes, that Ironjaw notices other furry creatures darting about although they keep their distance. He also realises there are two other dog soldiers crouched down watching them waiting for a command from the Lady.

'Is everything nocturnal?' Ironjaw asks.

'We are all creatures of the night here although some of us do inhabit the day as well,' she says.

The two outriders lead the way on a short journey down the mountain into a large crater, a great bowl of rock and ice, until they reach the flat ground at the bottom. There they find a tunnel entrance yawning open in front of them. Unseen from the edge of the crater it is big enough for both dragons to walk along it. Feeling the temperature getting milder they come to a massive chamber. In places water runs down its walls gathering in pools; emanating from several shafts in the floor is a curious blue green light.

They look at each other for a few seconds then Skadi explains,

'When we came here eons ago, we found strange places like this one which gave us shelter and helped us to survive. Let me hear your story now.'

Between them, the two dragons tell her of the lies the Darkness and Cravenclaw have been spreading about the Protectorship and particularly about who took the young dragons from Smorkis.

Skadi's eyes glitter dangerously, her anger growing with each word spoken. She says,

'We were told that the leaders of Horizon

would destroy what is left of us. The Black Dragon and the Darkness recruited some of us to do work for them; several we could ill afford to lose have been killed doing just that, two are still missing.'

'When I lost my children I came here first,' Smorkis explained. 'I had never bothered to visit before and I found these ones who were truly kind to me. Much later when I returned to the Winter Planet I found Cravenclaw was there. He was very sympathetic and understanding about my loss, telling me he knew who the culprits were, and why did I not join him in the fight as we had the same enemies. He seemed very sure of himself. The Darkness was very encouraging too, whispering to me that together we would eventually find my young ones alive.'

She looks at Skadi,

'That is, until I met the human female Lottie whose alter self is a white dragon. I have never met such a brilliant one as that before. I kept quiet about your existence as I promised and brought Ironjaw here so you could be convinced that what I say is the truth.'

'Contrary to what you might think we have no desire to fight anyone except to defend our independence,' Skadi says. 'There has been enough fighting in our past that has nearly destroyed us. We have hidden in strange places for hundreds of years and at last we begin to grow; our children begin to thrive. Then the Darkness came to be our friend but left a spy. She is sharp eyed, streaming across mountains, hiding in the craters to watch and wafting through the petrified forests. This is a small moon and she covers all of it. She is not like other ghosts. She carries a dark sword which is hot and burns if it touches you, she is the Darkness's creature, a wraith of ice and snow.'

'I will kill her for you.' Ironjaw says.

'You have the power?' asks Smorkis.

The Red Dragon nods his great head,

'Indeed, I do.'

'She will not let you close enough.' Skadi says.

'Then she has to come to me. She will have to make a report to her master so she will come to check what is happening. It is important she has not seen us already.'

'I don't think so,' Skadi replies.

'Then all we need is patience and a suitable place.'

Sometime later, Ironjaw is to be found crouched down on a flat plain of snow not moving, his eyes closed seemingly asleep. Nothing happens for several hours, then a low guttural bark breaks the silence followed by another, then another. The wind begins to increase and it starts to snow again.

The Dog Soldiers creep out of cover circling warily around him. There are more sharp barks signalling alarm. Eventually one or two venture closer. The Dragon does not move, he seems to be breathing very slowly and rhythmically, as though he has been somehow caught outside in the cold weather and gone into a kind of hibernation. He has wounds that look like they have come from a recent fight.

The Winter Wraith comes, her attention drawn by the intermittent barking, so she flows around a group of frozen trees some distance away watching. The Snarkles ignore her presence and continue to check the dragon. One jumps up on him but he does not stir. Eventually they decide to leave disappearing into the white wilderness. The snow is being turned into a blizzard by the wind, which begins to howl as the Wraith watches Ironjaw. Three of four hours pass, he does not move and eventually she too disappears into the landscape.

A day later Ironjaw is a great hump still lying there unmoved with the snow blowing over him. The Dog Soldiers keep coming to look at him. Skadi comes once, going right up to the dormant dragon but still he does not move. Smorkis turns up later accompanied by Skadi. She nuzzles him, tries roaring, breathes over him and pushes but nothing happens.

She tells Skadi speaking loudly,

'Something is very wrong here, he is alive but not alive; it must be a deep piece of black magic and I have no idea when, or if he will wake from it. We will have to bring others here to break the spell.'

Skadi nods her head and they move away wondering aloud which magician they should summon to help.

The Winter Wraith watches and listens, she has infinite patience but now they have mentioned others coming her master will have to know what is happening. She now knows this is one of his greatest enemies. She waits a little longer then flows slowly forward approaching the Red Dragon from the rear, giving him plenty of room as she warily circles around. He doesn't move, except unseen two eyelids flicker and the Dragon's eyes become very narrow slits.

The Wraith comes behind him again and jabs her sword into his skin which has little effect on such a hard surface, so she moves slowly, carefully to the front of him. Realising this is a chance to kill one of her Master's greatest enemies, she rises herself up intending to stab him in his eye. It is a mistake. His eyes suddenly snap open, his head lifts, his mouth opens, and he breathes out a huge sigh that freezes her quickly followed by fire spurting from his mouth. Completely surprised by the magical fire she has no chance of escaping it. The fire consumes her and in seconds she is gone without trace.

Ironjaw stands up and stretches. He cannot resist a great roar of triumph and those that hear it know they are free from being watched and spied upon. Skadi lopes alongside Smorkis across the snowy plain towards him knowing all has changed for the dog soldiers. Others may come but they now know their enemy.

28: A MURDER
OF CROWS

After the battle Lottie, Jack and Rodrigo make their way up to the cave to try to wake Rhea. She is still in a deep sleep as they gather around, talking to her, gently shaking her shoulder. Gretchen tries to wake her by breathing on her, apart from a slight fluttering of the eyelids it seems to have little effect. Both Rodrigo's and Jack's faces are taut and serious as they watch Lottie trying to enter the dreamtime yet again to follow the mystic path that has become a part of her. She sits on a nearby rock gently rocking backwards and forwards, her eyes closed to concentrate and search for her mother.

Eventually in her mind a long foggy corridor appears, undecipherable whispers start to come to her from unknown voices as she enters walking slowly. Shafts of light flash intermittently before speeding up, becoming a whirling pool of colour that spins her around, sucking her down into its depths. As it begins to slow, Lottie manages to break free to find she is suddenly flying above a valley where Rhea is lying in a meadow beneath an ancient oak tree. The branches are filled with hungry black crows cawing at her mother. They are waiting for her to fail as with her eyes closed and unable to see she tries to get up. Lottie becomes the White Dragon, roaring out her cold burning heat as she comes to land by her Mother's side.

It changes nothing. The crows rise swiftly from the tree as the fire bursts from her, circling away out of reach before they come rushing in again as soon as Lottie's attention is drawn to her mother.

'I am here! I am here!' She calls urgently to this woman she has never spoken to before.

Rhea hears her, but her eyes though now open are sightless as she tries yet again to find the strength to stand up holding onto the tree. She gets so far then her legs buckle and she slides back down again. Weak from continuously trying to wake up through the black magic that Typhon has breathed into her she is losing the battle. The crows wait for her to lie still.

Lottie in the dreamtime is getting desperate, something prevents her from helping her mother up. Although her fire gets through to the crows, it is as though there is an invisible force field that she herself cannot get past. It circles around Rhea as tightly as any rope might do. One or two of the crows drop from the branches to peck at her. Lottie roars at them and they fly up. The cawing gets louder, so she blows her fire making the crows rise quickly upwards only to return yet again. They know it cannot be long before Rhea's will to survive is exhausted.

Lottie calls desperately for others to join her. Jack, Rodrigo and Chingis are not hearing her and are not coming to help. It is left to someone else to do that.

There is a movement amongst the birds, a messenger comes, a much larger crow with piercing orange eyes. The other crows grow gradually quieter, grumbling, as she lands on a branch to hop briefly from foot to foot cawing loudly at them. The smaller black feathered birds bunch closer together, then as one start to rise above the interloper ready to strike. The large crow glares at them for a moment with her fierce eyes, then shaking her feathers lifts off to swoop down from the great tree bursting into blue flames as she goes. The Bird whizzes around the tree and Rhea, before soaring upwards towards her adversaries like a burning arrow. Flames shoot from her beak and the smaller birds scatter, screeching and cawing as they disappear. The Firecrow lands again to repeat the same peculiar little dance that she did when she arrived.

Lottie is transfixed by what she is seeing, and slowly by the base of the tree an image comes shimmering into being. The Gatekeeper is there wielding the Sword of Light which she points straight at Rhea's heart and gently stabs downwards. Almost immediately there is a moment of release, that smile begins to appear as Rhea turns her head towards Lottie and starts to stand up.

The images fade away like a tide going out as Lottie comes back from the dreamtime to the cave where Rhea is stirring. Her eyes opening slowly fill with amazement as she stretches out a hand for Jack and Lottie to hold.

'You are real,' she whispers, 'I heard you calling.'

Then she notices Rodrigo standing there and says,

'At last we are together. I have waited so long, hoping through the darkest and most tortured times that this moment would come.'

They are all smiling with relief although Rhea looks weak and very tired. Rodrigo says,

'You are safe now and should sleep for a while to gain some of your strength back. Then we can talk.'

Several hours later after they have all rested the twins and Rodrigo return. Rhea is sitting up looking a little better and stronger, sipping some cool clear water.

'I want so much to hear all about you two, every last detail but I think there will be plenty of time later. First we must find Ambrose,' she says, smiling at her children who smile back shyly.

'Yes, you are right we can wait,' Lottie says, 'What we need to know now is some background about you and our father, particularly how you were both captured as it may help to rescue him.'

Rhea smiles at them nodding her head in agreement.

'Well, your father came out of the sunlight and shadows of the enchanted woodlands called Brycea, a place on a mountainside on the planet of Mythra. Ancient ones of his people would gather, great mysteries would be discussed and memories shared.

'Ambrose's father was a forester who knew the ways of nature well. As a boy Ambrose would run with other children playing games through the woods. Later as he grew up, he would also wander among the elder ones gathering there watching and listening. Eventually, he began to take part in debates, where gradually it became recognised that he had an extraordinary gift of inner sight and vision. These peaceful people watched with alarm the coming of the Interventionists in the Galaxy, and they began to look at ways to defeat them.

'How did you both meet?' Lottie asks gently.

For a moment Rhea's eyes grow distant then she says,

'He arrived on our central planet Alpha, a young mystic, a scientist and a warrior ready to fight against the stupidity of the Interventionists. Their madness was at its height. Your father rose quickly to become famous, forming the Society of Protectors before being joined later by his brother in the fighting.

She smiles at Rodrigo, who says,

'He is older than me, and although we were close I knew less of my brother's early years after he left for Alpha. Later, after I arrived, I watched Ambrose become the main reason the unnecessary ones were defeated and have disappeared to the outer reaches of Horizon. He found the way to give some of us Protectors the ability to change shape and wear the skin-tight flexible armour that we have. He found the Dragon Sword and wore its ring before it was stolen.'

'Spellman found it and wears the ring now,' Jack interrupts to say. 'but that is another story.'

'Well Ambrose saved my life with it,' continued Rhea. 'We were fighting on the planet of Langamar, a planet of fire and rain where there were all kinds of weird and dangerous beings invented by those wishing us the greatest harm. It was a meeting that changed both our lives.'

29: RHEA AND AMBROSE

A long time ago on a deep and wide lake, a small fishing boat with just enough breeze to fill the sail cleaves its way silently through the calm water. The dawn's early light reveals that a boy has the rudder, steering it across the deep waters following the shoreline a hundred metres away. Lying in the brow is a warrior dressed in a dark coloured suit of the Protectors, a tough flexible material that allows maximum movement. At his side in its scabbard is a sword with a beautifully jewelled handle shaped to fit snuggly into his hand, on his finger is the dragon ring.

Ambrose is a tall slender man, his fair hair tied in a warrior's top knot. He is scanning the shoreline with its dense forest that almost reaches the water's edge. At the same time, he keeps a wary eye out across the lake trying to penetrate its horizon. He is looking for the amphibious creature that is the black Sea–Dragon Shatoo.

'Quietly now,' he says to the boy, and then

pointing, 'look, further along there, see the break in the tree line. That is where he must come ashore, it looks like a corridor of broken trees and foliage.'

The boy holds up his hand and they both listen. Behind the forest they can hear the cries and shouts, the clash of metal on metal as Protectors battle with an army of the Interventionists.

'The fighting has started. He will surely come now, he will not be able to resist it,' Ambrose murmurs to himself. 'He must be stopped or many will die. We will lose this fight if he is not killed and that would give the Interventionists an even greater heart to carry on.'

The boy hears and nods his head as Ambrose looks towards him,

'It has to stop Edwin. He has already killed many of us and is almost as dangerous as Cravenclaw himself.'

Edwin looks up at the man he would model himself on,

'If anyone can, you can. You have the sword and will succeed,' he whispers.

Just as the boy stops talking they are shown how dangerous the waters are. Almost without a ripple a shoal of long brightly coloured Biting-Fish appear. Their mouths filled with razor sharp teeth are snapping open above the water. For several minutes they swirl around the small boat before shifting off to look for other prey. The two in the boat watch them disappear.

Ambrose's eye is caught by a movement near the forest. A patrol of Protectors is running along the shore.

'Look there,' he says, 'they must be circling around to get behind the enemy, to come through the woods at them.'

A tall woman is leading the large group which is so intent on their purpose they don't notice the boat. He watches as they become the bait to catch a dragon, because moments later Shatoo explodes out of the water. A magnificent monster, he has a thick long scaly body pulsating with force and power. Dripping with water he takes to the air. His wings beat hard as he hovers above the runners, his fierce merciless eyes glaring down at them before a belch of fire snakes out to consume two of the soldiers nearest to him. Immediately he lunges down amongst them roaring and biting sending some of them skittling down.

Ambrose shouts,

'There Edwin! Land me just there!'

He points to a rocky outcrop.

The boy skilfully steers towards it, drifting in close for Ambrose to leap ashore. The Warrior draws his sword as he hurtles down the beach, his tall slender body crouched forward his long legs pumping into the wet sand. He can already see there is a circle of dead and dying Protectors. Shatoo has his teeth firmly gripped around the throat of a soldier that he lifts from the ground and shakes hard breaking his neck.

The leader is shouting,

'Into the trees, get into the forest where we have more chance of escape!'

She is putting herself in front of the Dragon trying to distract it while the others turn to run. His tail whips round smashing into her, sending her flying to land some distance away on the shore. He jumps after her to stand over his prey, then just as he is about to strike he looks up to see Ambrose. He is a short distance away shouting and running straight for him. Shatoo sends a gout of fire at the warrior who swerves to get out of the way.

Immediately the dark-haired woman rolls away to spring up and stab at the Dragon's side. It is only a painful pin prick to the great creature, nevertheless it creates a roar of anger as he turns back towards her. She runs somersaulting away from him like an athlete, to come up standing sword at the ready. Ambrose piles in wielding the Dragon Sword, managing to thrust it into his foreleg where it crunches against the bone causing blood to spurt out in a fountain.

The Sea-Dragon screams as it turns towards

him, but he is dancing away spinning and weaving, taunting the Dragon, laughing, telling him he is too slow and is not fit to be with others of the Black. The creature's eyes blaze as he takes a breath ready to blow fire. The woman Protector runs to jump up on his back. Scrabbling to get a hold, she manages to make several swipes at one of his wings and again the Dragon feels the sharp pin pricks and shrugs her off. Ambrose quick to take advantage dashes in to stab his sword into its side; this time it really hurts causing the creature to slump to one side.

Shatoo realises this man is different, the sword he carries will kill him. Seeing the two of them facing him on either side he inhales deeply to blow his fire, but they are ready for it diving away then coming at him from each side. He rises his wings to beat the air as he turns to leave them.

'No!' Shouts Ambrose. 'He must not get away!'

The Sea-Dragon hovers for a moment. It is a mistake. There is a glint of metal in the sunlight as the Dragon Sword spins through the air turning over and over. Thrown by Ambrose in a desperate attempt to stop Shatoo escaping, it lands with a thud cleaving its way into his throat and slicing his windpipe. Shatoo, his wings spread glides towards the lake, blood dripping, to splash down and thrash about fighting for air. It is a fight he cannot win and soon he becomes still as the last tremors shake his great body.

As he begins to sink, a small sailing boat swoops in and Edwin leans over its side to grab the hilt of the Dragon Sword. At first it looks as though he will be pulled under the water, but he manages to work it loose until it comes free. Shoals of Biting-Fish arrive as he gets out the oars and pulls hard for the shore.

Ambrose looks at the woman beside him as they go to greet the boy and retrieve the sword. She is nearly as tall as he is, he notices the scar down one side of her face near her ear.

'What's your name?' he asks.

'I am Rhea,' she replies.

'Ambrose,' he says, holding out his hand.

'Oh, I know who you are,' she says laughing and shaking his hand.

'Do you? How?

'You are quite famous you know,' she says with a smile.

For a moment he holds her eyes as Edwin comes hurrying up with the Dragon Sword. They are both congratulating him on his bravery when there are shouts and the sound of fighting coming from the edge of the forest. The remaining Protectors are engaging a group of Metalions.

'Take the boat back to your father. Tell him I am very grateful for the loan of it and of you.' Ambrose says smiling. 'I will visit soon.'

The two warriors run up the shore to help hold the line against the lumbering monsters. It is a hard fight because there are more Metalions than Protectors and they are strong, but they are also slow. They are supported by strange, winged bat like flying creatures with sharp teeth and talons that look like flying gargoyles. They make a yelping noise as they try to land on the shoulders of their opponents to bite into their necks. Wraiths shift in and out of the battle doing little damage except keeping up a constant howling.

Ambrose and Rhea begin to fight together, watching each other's backs as they cut a wedge into the enemy. Other Protectors, some wounded by the Sea-Dragon fight bravely by their side. Suddenly, an arrow thuds into one of the flying creatures which falls from the sky with a shriek. More shouting is heard and through the forest comes Adeth, leading his warriors and crashing into the back of the Metalions. The fight is over quickly with only a few of the metal soldiers managing to escape.

Ambrose and Rhea look at each other smeared in blood, sweating and panting from their exertions. For a few moments Rhea is taken over by this man with his fierce yet handsome face grinning at her, slapping her on the back and shouting,

'We should do that again sometime. What a fighter you are. We would be invincible!'

30: A FOOTFALL ON THE STEP

Rhea is speaking quietly,

'After the fight with Shatoo we fought many times together as comrades, and then came a sudden realization, a knowledge which made everything sharper, more in focus, colours brighter, feelings deeper. There was a strange and mysterious sense of belonging, as though we had known each other long before this time. We talked for hours.

'I have some learning and a little of the dreamtime talking is in me. However, Ambrose's knowledge grew. He became a magician, although he laughed when I called him that, nevertheless he did seek different codes and rhythms to life in the secrets and whispers of the Universe. We had many good friends who thought like us, Sebastian, Lillian, Adeth, Chingis, Ironjaw, the spider Morganast to name a few, and of course Rodrigo. And then came Darius.

'Ambrose found Darius as the tide began to fully turn against the Interventionists. You will have no doubt heard he was wandering lost, after Cravenclaw with others of his clan wiped out his wife and children in a raid. He was severely damaged emotionally and incoherent, so Ambrose brought him home. By then we were married and he became part of us as we tried to heal his loss and rehabilitate him. He quickly repaid us by becoming a great warrior. He was at the battle where Cravenclaw was captured, where Ambrose really discovered his magical abilities after the Dragon Sword was stolen. He overcame the Black One by force of will but he could not kill him. Later you were both born and we felt complete.'

There is a pause, and although they had heard some things about Ambrose from Rodrigo, it was quite different hearing it from Rhea. Lottie and Jack don't move, watching their Mother's every expression. Rhea takes a sip of water then continues,

'Less than a year after you were born the agony came. We were incredibly happy, we had you two and the war was virtually over so we could start rebuilding Horizon. We had been back to Mythra which had managed to stand firm against the Interventionists, and to Brycea which is truly enchanting, particularly when the warm breezes blow through the old trees bending their boughs a little. You expect to find unicorns in every glade.'

'We have the Wind Horses now.' Jack grins.

Rhea laughs,

'Exactly so.'

She continues with the story,

'Ambrose and Darius had become almost insep-arable. One day Darius suggested they go to visit the deep Labyrinth of Kume on the Planet Lang-amar where Ambrose and I first met in battle. The planet had been lost to us for many years so no one knew quite what to expect. However, Dar-ius had heard another Black Dragon was holed up there causing much grief by killing and raiding. Ambrose was also keen to go to see the Labyrinth, so Darius picked some trusty Protectors and away they went. That was the last I saw of your father.

'Darius returned a day or so later with shocking news. The dragon was defeated but Ambrose was missing. After the creature was driven off, escap-ing before it could be killed, Ambrose decided to have a look into the Labyrinth and simply didn't come back. Darius and the Protectors searched the cave passages for hours but found nothing.

'I was frantic with worry and decided to go my-self to see this place, although Darius, great friend that he was, felt it might be too dangerous and was against me doing that. In the end to appease me he decided to come with me.'

'But why didn't you tell me?' said Rodrigo.

'Yes, I realise I should have done, however everything happened so quickly. We thought, just for what would be a day or so we would keep it quiet to prevent any alarm. Anyway, I went with the group of them back to the Labyrinth. Part of the planet was still volcanic and unstable, but the Labyrinth was in the fertile part where it rained a lot.

'I remember that day; it was dark with thunder and lightning flashing in the distance but it stayed dry. I decided to enter alone as it had already been searched twice by the Protectors so I felt safe. I felt that Ambrose would have left me some sign, some message, and I needed to be quiet to see if I could hear it or find it.

'I took a flaming torch and set off down large echoing passages. There was evidence of the Black Dragon's recent occupation but also of others before that. Darius's group had done a good job of marking the way around, and there were infrequent burning torches along the corridors. I must have wandered for perhaps twenty minutes seeking some sign of your father and trying to enter the dreamtime. I eventually came to a set of wide steps hewn in the rock face that went upwards, so I started to climb.

'Then it came, the first time I felt something. It was an overriding sense of danger, a horrible shivery creeping feeling of evil. I remember stopping for a moment to turn around and listen. There was nothing to hear, although it felt as though the very shadows caused by the dancing torch flames were pressing in on me. I started to move on upwards.

'Then, after a short time, I realised that as I stepped up, there was a soft sound of a footstep mimicking mine. Every time I took a step, directly behind me there was another soft footfall, the slightest of echoes. I turned quickly and standing there lit up in the torchlight was a tall being in a black habit. I could not see its face, as it reached its arms towards me flames sprung from its bony hands. I stepped back in surprise and fright as a blackness came swirling around and the torch immediately sputtered out. The next thing I knew I was in a different place.'

Rhea looked up at Rodrigo who was watching her with a profoundly serious and grave expression on his face.

'You must have searched that Labyrinth for Ambrose and for me many times Rodrigo.'

Shaking his head, he replies,

'It is the first I have heard of it. I don't think any of the Council have ever heard of the Labyrinth of Kume either.'

There is a stunned silence broken by Jack,

'But that means...' he starts to say, but Lottie puts a hand on his arm,

'Let's just hear the rest of the story for a moment.'

Rhea stares at Rodrigo who looks shocked and angry,

'Lottie is right, let's hear the end of the story,' he says.

'I awoke sitting in a chair and having no idea how long I had been unconscious; I realised very quickly things had been taken from me. I could not transport myself or change from other than I am. My hands were tied. The room was light, there was a window and sitting on a large wooden chair by a table was the figure in the black robe. It was the only time it has ever spoken directly to me which it did with such loathing, such hate and malice, its voice hard but filled with pleasure. It said to me,

"I will make sure you have just enough left to witness the destruction of Horizon, the death of your friends, your children and of course Ambrose. Exquisite tortures that will drive you mad because you will be powerless to do anything about it. We will strip you of all those minor powers you think so great, although I will give you an insight into what real power can do. Ambrose will be broken when he hears you are in my company. I will take your children too, perhaps they will become mine."

'I struggled against the ropes, trying to stand, trying to get at this creature although I had no weapon. I shouted out that he would never succeed, we would always win however long it took.

'There was no cackling laughter, nor any demonic shouting. I just had a feeling I was facing a force that was implacable and now bathing in a deep, evil satisfaction. Yet, there was something I thought I recognised in this creature which just slowly shook its head at me. The air shifted and it was gone replaced by the Darkness, ready to start a battle of wills as it tried to wash away my senses and skills to change who I was. It was agony, but they let me keep some cognitive elements so they could torture me with images of their wicked deeds.

'I was not completely weakened. I managed to keep some senses locked away that would allow some autonomous thought. I was given a drug to keep me compliant and kept hidden by being moved around from place to place until I became a prisoner with the Sylli. It was obvious that they did not approve of this devil, whose name I now understand is Typhon. Between us we duped him as to how much he thought he was controlling me.'

Rhea paused then said,

'I have no idea where Ambrose is, we must find him.'

'Have you met Magda Cross?' Jack asks.

Rhea's face hardens,

'Oh yes, Magda Cross was particularly over-joyed to show me the deaths of Sebastian and Lillian. I will never be able to thank them now for keeping you safe. I will never forgive her for that.'

Lottie tries to say something but the words won't come. Tears prick her eyes which are mirrored in those of her mother and brother. For the first time Rhea and her children hug each other tightly. Rodrigo puts his hand on Rhea's head before walking out of the cave, his eyes flint hard, his face savage. He now knows who the traitor is, a spy for the Darkness and the evil Typhon, who will have stolen the Dragon Sword and who has tried to kill them all.

31: LORD OF THE LEAVES

While Rhea is talking on the Winter planet, back on Earth Agnes the Witch is moving as silently as she can through a wood of ancient oak trees. Her senses are acutely tuned to a threat of danger which seems to pervade the very foliage. In the sun the tree shadows are a mystery, it is as though something lurks unseen, following her. Agnes often stops to look around yet everything appears to be normal. Since finding Willow she has felt watched, her movements tracked but never as strongly as this. She is heading for Eda's hideout turning and twisting through the trees disguising the way, doubling back on herself checking that no one is there.

Until that is, she comes to a very lonely place where a stream is bubbling through the forest glade where Magda Cross stands beneath a pinnacle of rock. The Witch stops still, her heart thumping.

Magda Cross is stunning, her dark hair shines in

the sunlight while on her beautiful face there is a beaming smile,

'Come my dear, I have been waiting for you. It is good to have you all to myself. Come, step forward.'

Agnes looks about her for an escape from a certain and probably agonising death.

'I wouldn't consider it, there is nowhere you can run. I will surely catch you and you are to be completely mine now. You have let me down, turned away from my friendship and helped my enemies. We will show them all what that means. How long and painful a path it is to soothe my anger.'

The beautiful image slips as her eyes glow red and her long tongue curls out from her mouth.

For a moment the light seems to dim as Agnes steps forward trying to clear her mind, to call upon nature itself in the forlorn hope it will help her. This human being looks at the things she loves, the whisper of a breeze in the leaves, the thrush's song, the touch of the earth beneath her, the stream that endlessly runs its course. Her mind gulps with the sadness of going away from it,

'I call you to rise if you are here. I call you by your hidden name. Wildvine, Lord of the Leaves come to my side, let the forest protect me,' she whispers slipping to the ground unable to move another step. Her eyes close as she faints away.

'That will not help you,' laughs her enemy.

Magda Cross's attention is drawn by a movement of the forest elements that are slowly shifting about. Part of the foliage, the green bushes
their branches entwined, the long grass, the
mossy earth is rising into a shape that is human-
like as it grows. Birds fly to land on it, bees buzz in
its flowers. It moves towards the evil woman.

Magda Cross waits patiently, a cruel smile on
her face. She asks,

'Tell me your name, what are you called?'

'I am the Lord of Misrule,' he sighs, 'Captain of
the upside-down world, King of small things. You
are not wanted here in my place.'

Magda Cross claps her hands in delight,

"Ah I have heard of you; it is interesting that the
Witch can call on you, although my Master is so
much stronger than you can ever imagine. You are
just leaf and branch, a tree being, one of the leaf-
born and you are too old to upset what fate has
been cast for this one. I will burn you up like kind-
ling wood.'

A curious change comes as the bright green
turns to black, to grey and then to air to be filled
by the softly sighing voice.

'You think you can change the nature of things.
My dear you have no idea what you say, I am all
around you. The right words spoken are powerful

and I have been called. Nothing about you that I can see is foretold, nothing is written down, you are not mentioned in any future pages that I can turn. Perhaps you should move away from the path you walk.'

Magda Cross changes. The chimera standing on her back legs breathes fire and roars, her two heads spinning around to look every way for this being she has disturbed.

The voice is at her ears chuckling,

'Oh, dear me, you really don't know anything.'

The air shifts and in front of her is a green dragon, tall, almost elegant, that wastes no time before battering into Magda Cross with an awful strength that sends the Chimera reeling. Recovering she takes to the air spitting fire, her tail lashing but the green dragon disappears to be replaced by clouds of small flying insects. They fly to blind her; some get burned up in her fire but there are many more of them. She crashes to the floor. Immediately getting back up, incensed, boiling with rage she finds facing her is a large beautiful butterfly, its delicate wings interwoven with red and blue. She hurries towards it ready to kill, but the fragile creature's tongue licks out spitting a sticky substance which covers her, enraging Magda Cross even more.

A wind comes shaking the leaves on the trees which fall silently, endlessly to cover the Chimera, sticking all over her as she tries to reach the exquisite insect. Of course, it has gone with the wind, in its place is a giant of a man. He is disabled, his back is bent, his hands twisted, one leg is obviously shorter than the other as he hobbles towards her carrying a wooden club. He is strong, the sunlight of the forest is in his eyes. He raises the club to smash her. Magda Cross's serpent head blows a gout fire which envelopes him and he disintegrates into a thousand small mice that run all over her biting, biting.

Magda Cross reels round and round, roaring out her fury trying to snap at them, blowing fire into the air, her poisonous tail thumping the ground, but it is a useless thing.

The Darkness comes to her whispering,

'Come away, come away.' Enveloping her it caresses her pain, soothes her ego. 'Now is not the time, later all will be avenged.'

Sometime later Agnes opens her eyes to look up at the blue sky; an animal is nudging her leg making a snuffling noise, its breath hot on her flesh. She looks up as one of Eda's guardians backs away and trots off to find its master.

32: EYES ACROSS THE STREET

While the battle on the Winter Planet is being fought Christine and Sergio are continuing to run the farm as usual. The Wild Ones, Agnes and Willow make secret visits to watch over them. Willow, wherever she goes always returns to stay behind the waterfall.

One morning the two of them decide to go for supplies in the local town where it's market day. It is a lovely spring day with almond trees beginning to blossom, soon large areas of the mountains will be transformed by flowering trees.

When they arrive, the stalls are already busy selling clothes, rugs, flowers, plants and all manner of produce in a square off the main street. Opting to sit outside one of the many bars in the sunshine for a coffee, they watch the towns people and tourists go about their business for a while. There is much talking and catching up with neighbours who have come into town from all over the area, Sergio and Christine are caught up in the normalcy of it all. There is not a dragon or a metal monster anywhere to be seen, although Sergio looking up does catch sight of Bonny circling around high up in the blue sky.

After a while, Christine notices she is being watched from a café across the street by a tall man, who having just paid his bill was waiting for change and staring at her. It wasn't unpleasant, in fact it was obviously a look of admiration. She coloured up slightly and smiled which was returned a little cautiously. A passing friend distracted her for a few moments so that when she looked again the proprietor was wiping the table and the man had gone.

They decide to split up, Sergio going off to the ironmongers and then to the stall selling shoes to buy a pair of new boots. Meanwhile, Christine drives the truck to the supplier's yard to buy some bags of concentrated food for the horses and sheep. Business is brisk and soon she is backing the vehicle up to a barn door where there are several high stacks of bags of animal feed. Tying back her long auburn hair, she reaches up to lift the first of the ten bags she needs from the top of the stack. She could reach it but as she turns away, a sack from the next and higher stack slides forward knocking her to the floor and winding her.

As she tries to get up, a passer-by, the stranger from the café rushes in to help her. Afterwards she was to describe him as tall, with flowing hair, a face with a slightly hooked nose and stunning eyes, a term which made Sergio smile broadly. The stranger helps her to her feet, and while she leant against the side of the barn trying to get her breath, promptly loaded the truck with the required sacks. He turns to ask if she is alright, taking her arm to help her into the cab. She says in her lilting welsh voice,

'Yes, I'm fine now thank you. Are you from around here?'

'No, I am just passing through,' came the soft toned reply, 'travelling around this area for a while.'

They looked at each other; there was something she couldn't read in his face, his eyes looked puzzled and slightly alarmed yet he was friendly.

'I'm Christine. What's your name?' she asked holding out her hand.

For a moment there was a pause as though he was thinking about it which she put down to shyness. Then he awkwardly shook her hand and said his name was David.

'Well David, can I buy you lunch as a thanks for helping me?' she said, realising she was about to invite him to the farm and how impossible that would be.

He had recovered himself and replied gallantly,

'I need no reward from you, and I am afraid I

have to move on elsewhere just for a while.'

"OK,' she said starting the engine. 'Perhaps see you around when you're back. Thank you again.'

The truck drove off as the Harlequin raised his hand in farewell.

Christine picked up Sergio and they headed back to the farm. A journey in which, after telling him about the stranger she has to endure a certain amount of teasing. Finally, he got that look which meant he might be walking back if he continued. When they got to the farm such frivolity was forgotten. Agnes is waiting for them with a warning.

'They are back, my Sisters have seen them.'

'Who is?' Christine asks.

'The Metalions, several off them with Dynasta their leader. They were seen last night near a ruined and deserted olive mill about ten kilometres from here, there is no sign of any of the others yet.'

Later after unloading they sit around the table in the sun listening to Agnes talking, trying to explain her confrontation with Magda Cross. Before either of them gets to ask questions, Willow arrives with news of the fight on the Winter Planet, Jacks capture and release, the escape of the evil ones and the rescue of Rhea. All of which she has watched from a distance, leaving after Rhea was helped from the cave.

'Wow, they got away from the fight just like last

time,' says Christine.

'Yes,' Willow replies, 'and there is a new horrible entity, the most mysterious and frightening I have seen, in fact, absolutely terrifying. A huge human-oid creature came out of the Darkness to stand in front of them. The Darkness fawned around it for a while, then it rose into the air like a great black curtain and as before, when it rolled away they were all gone.'

Agnes updates her on events at the Olive Mill. After a slight pause Willow says,

'I think Rhea and the others will be back soon. Meanwhile we should be concerned with events at the old Mill. Will all those that escaped be coming back here to meet and regroup I wonder?'

'Let's take a look,' says Christine looking at Willow.

'Yes,' says Sergio looking at them both, 'I agree we should check it out.'

A plan is made not to wait for the others but to go there that very night. Agnes heads off to warn Eda and the Wild Ones.

Across the mountains not so far away, Archie the youth with the eye patch is getting bored and a little petulant. In the furore of the last days it would seem everyone has forgotten him. Magda Cross thinking to keep him safe has sedated him for prolonged periods of time. Although he wants to please her, he is becoming stubborn and his training is not going well.

Archie's past is a disaster; brought up in various institutions and with several foster parents, he resisted all authority and was eventually left to rot. He became a petty criminal, with a first short prison sentence for breaking and entering into several houses. His loss of an eye and leg injury are the result of a motorbike accident on a stolen machine.

Harlequin who he likes is the only person he has seen for the last two days. Two damaged souls, they are talking together whilst walking a little way around the mountain.

'I am fed up with this,' he is complaining, 'Where is she? I do the best I can. I saw the Wolf in Bristol and what was all that about? I listen to what she says about how I will reap the benefit of being with her, but nothing happens.'

To stave off any more complaining Harlequin asks him how he met his so-called mother. Archie smiles grimly,

'I broke into her house by the lake. I had been sleeping rough for a few days in an old barn in the hills and was starving, cold and broke. I had seen the car come and go and reckoned there would be food and some things in there I could steal to sell. Needs must I suppose. Anyway, one night with the car gone I forced one of the back doors and got in.

It was a very well-furnished house, but weird because there wasn't any food or drink anywhere except water in the tap. However, there was a bathroom with a bath and hot water and I couldn't resist it. She found me sound asleep in the bath. I awoke to find her sitting quietly watching me.

'She was kindness itself, said she needed a helper, asked me about myself then said she could show me another life. Kept calling me her son. I wasn't going to argue and here we are.'

'What about your real parents?' Harlequin asked.

'Never had any of those,' came the short reply.

'Well, you are going to have to be patient for a while longer that's all there is to it. When Magda Cross is back here then things will change,' says Harlequin as they wander on.

Harlequin is aware of the Metalions presence. They have arrived unexpectedly; something must have gone wrong. They will keep themselves hidden during the day. Tonight however no matter how much he dislikes them, he will have to speak with them to find out what is going on.

33: THIS IS MY FIGHT!

Dynasta is raging from the defeat on the Winter planet, his voice still a growl of hate when Harlequin questions him that evening to learn things have indeed not gone as planned. He has brought three of his foot soldiers to watch over the boy on the orders of Magda Cross. She, who is on her mission of revenge, will come soon to take him to another place in case he is discovered and she loses him.

As the massive metal monster talks to the tall slim man he would rather kill, the Darkness comes dancing across the rough terrain towards them. Again, the Dark Entity wraps them in promises of revenge and power, of the dark joy to be had in the demise of their enemies, of the loyalty to their Master that will bring them happiness and the power they crave. It sighs and soothes the angry Metalion and it exhorts the Harlequin to be ready for the coming battles. Then it spirals away appearing as though slightly mad and eccentric;

neither beings are fooled by its almost jaunty air, it is an utterly black soul and a killer.

Dynasta, his powerful hunched stance a night-time terror, a darker shape silhouetted against the night sky growls,

'For now human, for now you are safe from us, it will not always be so. I leave these other ones to help you guard the boy, they know what to do. I have other things to settle but I will be back shortly.'

The air moves and he is gone.

Eda, some way off, a very still night shadow against a rock, watches the exchange and the coming of the Darkness. His son Rezto slides away to find Sergio, Christine and Willow who are gathered further down the wide stony track to the old Olive Mill. Rezto reports,

'The largest Metalion has gone, although we think there may be three others around and there is a human, the one we saw at the meeting with Magda Cross and Cravenclaw. This afternoon one of our watchers spotted him walking around the mill with a youth wearing an eye patch.'

'So that's who they are guarding here, the boy that Jack saw,' says Christine. 'Magda Cross has captured another youngster to grow in her own image. She will give him extraordinary powers if she can, he will then be let loose to ingratiate himself and cause serious trouble.'

Sergio replies, 'If we are to get him now is our best chance. Who knows what will happen next? For sure, there will be more to guard him soon and he will no doubt be spirited away when the Chimera returns.'

'Now we know where he is we have little choice,' Willow agrees.

They all look at each other with grave and serious faces.

In the ruined mill the living accommodation has been made comfortable. Archie is sleeping on a bed having been given a drink that will knock him out for most of the night and day. The Harlequin watches his rhythmic breathing. He is surprised that he has become quite fond of the boy, recognising, although millions of light miles apart, a similar sad and savage upbringing. He shuts the door and wanders through the house and out into the air to sit on an old wall and look up at the stars.

The Dormouse slips past him, and in a trice is under the old door skipping along the corridors to find the sleeping Archie. She pauses for a moment, reconnoitres the room, slips back out under the door, looks in several other rooms which she finds are empty so dashes back outside. Willow goes to ground in a tuft of grass, and watches as the three Metalions arrange themselves in separate places around the mill to sit quietly on their haunches to wait out the night. It is a lonely place, very dark and nothing seems to be moving. The Mouse scuttles secretly away.

About an hour later, Harlequin is still contemplating the dark landscape when a soft glowing light appears below him. He can't quite make out what it is, but as he watches one of the Metalions lumbers slowly towards the light. Suddenly there is the sound of a fight going on and the great creature is thrashing around and grunting loudly. The Harlequin doesn't hesitate, he immediately runs for the house and Archie.

Below the Metalion is being attacked by about twenty Wild Ones, arrows flying as they run rings around it. Also, running across the ground come Eda's two guardians the enormous black boars. Their heads are lowered, their huge tusks pushed out as they crash into the Metalion's legs. As it totters, its long arms flailing around with sword and axe, they retreat a few metres to repeat the process and down it goes. Immediately the Wild Ones are all over it and its end comes quickly.

By now the other two are lumbering up to join in the fight, as perhaps a further fifty Wild Ones appear as though out of the ground to take them on in a similar way. The metal monsters' whirl around, their axes and swords occasionally finding their mark as they try to bat away their diminutive but fierce enemies, while the boars continue to hammer at their legs.

Meanwhile, Sergio and Christine have made it to the entrance. The old worn door is locked so Sergio steps back, lowers his shoulder and hammers into it. Bursting through they run to find the bedroom but Archie is gone. Racing through the house they eventually find the back door is swinging open. Chasing through it they are met with an empty night in which there is no movement just several clumps of trees gently waving in the breeze.

'We are going to have to split up,' Christine says.

Sergio is about to disagree but she is insistent,

'It's the only way. We can cover much more ground.'

'OK,' he says, 'but be careful.'

'You too,' she replies and off they go, one left and one right.

Christine finds them as she comes out of the nearest grove of trees. She sees a hunched figure carrying another over his back, trying to be as quiet as possible.

She rushes silently right up to them,

'Stop!' she calls, 'Over here Sergio, over here!'

The figure turns to look straight at her ignoring the gleaming sword she is pointing at him.

For a moment she is shocked but manages to utter,

'You,' she says.

Then he sees rising behind her a massive figure, its axe raised ready to strike.

'Look out!' he shouts, in one movement dropping Archie and launching himself at her, pushing her out of the way.

The sword cuts his arm as Dynasta with a roar, using his huge strength sweeps him away to hit his head against a tree. Christine raises her head from where she has fallen to see him sink to the ground and lie still.

Willow arrives with Sergio who immediately stands to face Dynasta. The air moves and a voice says,

'This is my fight!'

'Spellman,' breathes Willow.

'I have been looking for you,' the Warrior growls.

Dynasta, overjoyed to be facing Spellman, grunts,

'You at last. I have been waiting for this.'

The Protector makes no further sound as he faces the creature, lumbering with his powerful hunched gait towards him, axe and sword in hand. Spellman skips precisely and fast out of his way. Concentrating, his face grim and savage, he circles the Metalion making him turn and turn again. The massive creature roars with the frustration of trying to catch the fast-moving Protector. Spellman darts in, getting through his defence yet again to prick him with the Dragon Sword. The Metalion swings the axe downwards and lunges at him to no avail. It is not long before Dynasta with all the weight of metal he carries begins to tire, the great sword swipes he is making starting to slow.

Spellman is deadly, suddenly moving like lightning inside the waving axe and sword, stabbing the Dragon Sword through the metal deep into the creature's body. Dynasta falls to the ground where he struggles like a wounded animal to get back up again as blood spurts from his wound.

The Wild Ones having finished off the other Metalions come to circle around him and Spellman. The fearsome creature tries to move again, opening his mouth as though trying to speak, but the wound is fatal and he slumps back with a groan. Willow watching notices that there is almost a sense of relief in the creature's eyes as they close and he stops breathing.

'This is what our enemies were fully guilty of,' she says, 'making these mutations, these unhappy beings.'

'Yes,' says Spellman.

They all gather around Archie who still sleeps.

'OK, let's get him back to the van and on to the farm,' Sergio says.

'What about this one?' Spellman says, kicking Harlequin's boot.

'Wait, leave him alone,' says Christine kneeling beside Harlequin. 'He will have to come with us.'

34: TALKING WITH A TRAITOR

On the Winter Planet the thaw is fully set in with the snow and ice retreating, except on the highest mountain tops. The river is gushing across the plain, trees are in bud and flower, strange birds are singing, insects buzzing and the sun is hot. They are all back safely, including the three Hobi Rats Lennie, Caramel and Hannibal and the two Sylii Bano Escatara and Ederoy. Gathered on the mountain looking out towards the Ice Valley they watch it melting before their eyes.

Rhea looks around at them, saying

'I simply cannot find enough words to say thank you for maintaining your belief that I was still alive and for rescuing me. Even in the worst moments of my years of imprisonment, I clung on to the light that I know also shines in you. Perhaps now we can start to win back what has been lost.'

Looking at Caramel and Hannibal she continues,

'Without you two picking up my message and taking action, none of this would have happened and I would still be a prisoner.'

There are immediate nods of agreement and mutterings of 'hear hear' from the others, followed by a general shuffling of feet and harrumphing from the two Hobis.

"Where is Willow?' asks Rhea 'I would like to meet and thank her too.'

'Spellman has gone to find her. He thinks she is back on Earth,' says Branca.

Ironjaw looking towards Synabeth and Gretchen, suggests it might be a good idea to send them back to Earth for a while in case there is a need, a suggestion which is quickly accepted.

Rodrigo has told them all Rhea's story directly after exiting the cave where she and Jack were briefly held prisoner, and before they moved back across the plain. Now he says,

'We have a traitor that has been growing amongst us for many years. We have to decide what to do.'

'There can be no doubt?' asks Lottie.

'I think not. Darius was the only one who knew we were coming here, and we found Rhea was moved and our enemies waiting for us. He led Rhea to the Labyrinth where she met Typhon. The same probably happened to Ambrose as well. He set up Spellman and Rodrigo to be attacked by the She-Dragon Paedrenostra which resulted in the death of many Protectors.'

'And he and his companions did not tell you where I had gone to look for Ambrose and what happened. For one who was so close to us, that's not an act of a friend,' Rhea adds. 'It now looks as though his story of losing his wife and children is a lie.'

Rodrigo continues,

'He obviously ingratiated himself with Ambrose to become fully trusted, realising that the Interventionists were about to be finally defeated. He is completely fake and clever, going to ground, setting himself up as a 'sleeper' until such time as he could reveal who he was. While we have been fighting here on the Winter Planet, he was probably waiting on Alpha to take control had the outcome been the way he wanted it.'

There is a pause before he continues slowly,

'He was also there when the Dragon Sword was stolen, ensuring it would be almost impossible to kill Cravenclaw.'

There is a short silence then Jack asks,

'Who is he? What is he? He has betrayed us constantly, an imposter we should get rid of quickly.'

'I think we are all wondering about that. He is a traitor. What we don't know,' says Chingis, 'is he

the servant or the master? What is his relationship to that abomination Typhon and the Darkness? How deep has he embedded himself with
others, so that if we declare him traitor how many
may rise to help him? We should try to ascertain
that before rushing in to expose him.'

'Mm, I think you are right my friend,' Rodrigo
agrees. 'It was him that sought permission to raise
more Protectors, perhaps he now has a private
army. How we find that out is going to be difficult.'

'Well,' Rhea interrupts, 'if he thinks my memory has returned and I can expose him he will be
on his guard. Therefore, he needs to be told I still
have no recollection of what happened when I was
captured.

'Yes,' Rodrigo muses, 'we will need to ensure he
understands that.'

They all fall silent for a few moments thinking
it over.

Lottie says,

'Are you sure you told no one else Rodrigo?'

A pause then,

'Of course, I didn't. I went to see Adeth but
surely you don't think......'

'Absolutely not,' says Lottie, 'but it does open
the way to a plan we might try to implement, as
we watch, wait and make sure who our friends are.
It is important Darius does not think we know he

is traitor.'

They all look at her. Jack picking up on his sister's thoughts adds,

'Of course, we have to try to dupe him. He mustn't know we are on to him for a while. I would guess, with luck he has not had time to bind new Protectors to him, but it is not worth the risk of confronting him.'

Two days later, Darius is watching Rodrigo and Branca intently as they walk up the great hall to report about the battle on the Winter Planet.

'Brother,' he says, 'it is good to see you, and you too Sister.'

He has with him a Protector called Leeward, who is now one of his lieutenants, promoted to work closely with him. A slightly built human who always seems to have a sly look on his face. Darius considers him useful to the cause of rooting out supporters of the evil ones.

Standing near him is Vivienne, a striking looking woman who has partly webbed hands, yet her fingers are long. She is dark skinned with coal black pupils, her hair rides on her shoulders and she is dressed in the tough skin-tight all in one suit of the Protectors. She carries a long sword which hangs from her belt. Tall and muscular, she is a powerful shadow that rarely speaks. A look passes unnoticed between Vivienne and Branca, a recognition of each other.

Darius introduces them and Rodrigo answers with a greeting,

'It is good to see you as well and a pleasure to meet these two.'

Darius smiles,

'It seems there is some danger of me being assassinated,' he laughs. 'In my view very unlikely, however the council members have insisted so Vivienne has been appointed to the task of protecting me.'

Rodrigo tells them the story of the battle on the Winter Planet and the rescue of Rhea.

Darius gets to his feet seeming genuinely pleased,

'Well done. Well done this is excellent news.'

Rodrigo inclines his head accepting the praise.

'But there is a problem,' he says. 'We have a traitor, someone who knew we were heading for the Winter planet, had Rhea moved and attempted to trap us. Eventually we managed to wake Rhea who does not remember anything about what has happened to her unfortunately'

The eyes of the three of them are fixed on Rodrigo's face, while Branca watches for a reaction from Darius. He lowers his head for a moment masking his face as Rodrigo continues,

'I only told two people, you Darius and Adeth.

We know with your background you are very unlikely to be part of those who killed your own family.'

Both Branca and Rodrigo give brief smiles at the impossibility of Darius siding with the enemy.

'So, it has to be Adeth.'

Darius looks shocked,

'Can you prove that?'

'No, but it is possible. We don't know a great deal about his past, except he was very close to Ambrose and trusted. At the very least I suggest we have him watched.'

Darius says,

'We can certainly do that but tell me, is there any news of Ambrose?'

'There is none yet. As I said Rhea remembers nothing although we hope she will in time, so the search continues. Hopefully if one is alive perhaps the other one is too.'

'Yes, you should definitely continue with that. When will Rhea return here? I look forward to seeing her again. I owe her a lot.'

'She is weak but after some rest I am sure she will be eager to return.'

'Perhaps I might visit her.'

'Of course, in a week or so when she has recovered a little more,' Rodrigo replies.

They continue to talk for a while about watching the coming and goings at the house of Adeth before both Branca and Rodrigo take their leave.

Outside the building they pause,

'Well,' Rodrigo said, 'he played that very straight, but I wonder if he believes us? Have we done enough to make him feel safe for a while? I am not at all sure about the shifty looking Leeward, he never looks you in the eye, but Vivienne is interesting.'

'Ha Ha,' Branca claps her hands in delight. 'You liked her! Well brother I know of her, she is from the Fisher Folk and will be utterly loyal to Adeth. Her hair hides the small gills in her neck which she uses in water, she also has lungs, therefore like all her kind can breathe in two elements. Adeth, who we see now as an old man was a great warrior in his time. I think somewhere in the past he and the Fisher Folk fought together which has led them to highly respect him.'

'Well, a story for another time,' Rodrigo shrugs and smiles. 'I have spoken to Adeth secretly so he knows of the plan to try to deceive Darius. He told me that someone working for him is very close to Darius, obviously Vivienne. Have you met her before?'

'We have heard of each other and I fought beside her brother Ketill once. He is maybe an even better fighter than Spellman, although I doubt the dreadlocked one would agree,' Branca grins. 'Darius will know who she is but he will not gainsay a council decision, at least not yet. She will cramp his activities a little, just by being there most of the time.'

Much later that night Leeward slips away unnoticed to call a secret meeting.

35: CAT AND MOUSE

The Demon Naptha, temporarily forgotten by Magda Cross in the heat of battle, is a phantom of the night patiently watching and waiting. A loner, coming and going unseen he cares for neither side only for himself, although he wants Willow back to do his bidding as he was promised. He waited for her to come to him, until it became obvious that she had escaped his clutches to return to the light side.

He was there unseen searching for her at the battle on the Winter Planet. He saw Spellman kill Dynasta at the ruined Olive Mill, making his blue eyes glitter with anticipation, waiting for his chance to grab her away. His frustration is increased as Willow is never still, never anywhere on her own long enough for him to catch her. He cannot find where she hides.

'I will not rest until I get her back,' he mutters to himself. 'She will realise what we can be together. What power we can create for ourselves. If not she will die.'

Astride his horse with Black Dog at his side, he is watching now from a distance outside the ruined mountain fort where Archie and Harlequin have been taken. The old fort was used once before to hide Sebastian and Lillian after their rescue from the Tigari. The weather has turned, the rain coming in waves through the low clouds, it runs off him but he appears not to notice. He cannot get any nearer because he has spotted the two young red dragons standing like stone sentinels hidden on the mountainside.

Inside the cave at the back of the fort it is warm and dry. Christine is sitting on a rock by the Harlequin who is lying on the floor with his eyes still closed, while Sergio and Eda watch over Archie.

Willow and Spellman are at last able to talk to one another. As her guardian, Spellman has been in a difficult place trying to defend her actions and was excluded from her rehabilitation. Now he has had a first-hand account from her and is fuming, wanting to get at the Demon. She gives him a huge hug,

'We will have to bide our time for that, I am very aware that I am watched. Sometimes I can feel his presence and I have horrible dreams about the deaths of Sebastian and Lillian. I feel so guilty and only I can attempt to put it right.'

'No!' Spellman says raising his voice. 'Not on

your own, we do it together.'

Willow raises her head to look at him and smile,

'So be it,' she says.

Spellman turns away satisfied. Looking across the cave at Christine and the Harlequin, he says in a low voice to Willow,

'How did that happen?'

Willow chuckles quietly saying,

'If only we knew.'

'Mm but what do we do about it?' comes the reply.

'I don't know,' she says. 'Whatever it is it will have to wait. There is much to do, we need to be back on Alpha. I will tell the others. Jack, Lottie and Rhea are sure to return here soon to be with them.'

Forty-eight hours later the gathering begins on the lost planet of Langamar where Rhea and Ambrose first met. It is another fiery planet of small volcanoes, mountainous terrain, deserts and deep blue seas. Leeward's message has gone out and the night terrors willingly and eagerly transport themselves across the Galaxy. There are several representatives of each, among them are the giant centipedes called Tigari, as well as Owl-men, Metalions, the Black Dragons, Deathworms and the Shilocks. The huge dark green amphibious humanoid brother of Typhon is there, and the Wraiths that can do little but watch, point and howl.

They have all come in secret to cross the river to enter the mouth of the Palace of the Dead, a building hewn out of the rock as a burial chamber for the chiefs of a long-forgotten tribe. The Darkness is swirling around the Chimera Magda Cross. Cravenclaw watches the audience gather. There is an atmosphere of anticipation in the great fire lit cavern.

They watch as Darius steps up on a slab of rock. The air shimmers as he changes in front of them to become Typhon, the black cloaked hellion, the archfiend of evil.

'Be ready,' he says, 'Be ready, our time is close at hand. I can no longer stay hidden; they have finally seen me hiding among them. They pretend that Adeth is a traitor and seek to learn our strength. As if I would not see through that. I am Typhon, and they have no idea yet what I can do.'

With that the air shakes, transformation starts to take place, the black robed figure grows in front of them, something many of them have not seen before. His arms spread wide, fire in his palms spitting and crackling, his voice a loud whisper which echoes in their ears insistent and compelling; with it comes a force, a feeling of dreadful hate.

'We will have chaos and then we will have

power. You will have power. We will sweep the Universe to take our revenge, killing Ambrose and his children, defeating and ruining the Protectors. Then we shall look outward across the endless reaches of space to find whatever there is we can attack and make our own. Go back, tell your soldiers to be ready, the angels of the dark are coming, their wings will beat a tattoo in the air, their shrieks of black joy a battle cry. I will give you a demonstration of what I can do. I will strike right at their heart very soon.'

A murmur of excitement echoes around the cavern. A swirling, incessant, rhythmic beat of the tumbrels rising in power comes into their heads. The hypnotic driving beat is calling them, inspiring them, exhorting them to be open to the malice of the Darkness that flows around them and through their consciousness. It anoints their reason with hate and loathing, binding them, making them as one for the Master of Chaos.

Typhon, the devil creature is unaware that someone else is listening to his words. The Mouse, taking an insane risk travelled with him. Watching and waiting for her chance, the little creature saw Darius's coat hanging on a chair in the council chamber. Distracted by an animated conversation with Spellman he didn't notice what was happening as she climbed into one of his large pockets. There she curled into a soft ball of fur underneath a handkerchief.

Willow was out of his pocket in a trice to slip away into the great cavern to spy on proceedings before Darius changed to the black cloaked Typhon. Unfortunately, she has been spotted scurrying around in the shadows. Leeward transforms into a cat which starts to stalk its prey.

Willow is listening intently, appalled and shocked at the change in Darius to this dark and loathsome creature.

'Now that explains a lot,' she says to herself. 'Darius and Typhon are one and the same. He has for so many years pretended to be our greatest supporter while betraying us as often as he can.' She creeps closer to listen.

After Typhon stops speaking the others file out, leaving Magda Cross, Cravenclaw and the Darkness with the Master who bends to look straight at the Chimera,

'You have let us down,' he says calmly. 'Your fixation on the child has caused the death of three Metalions and of Dynasta. You and Cravenclaw both lost the battle on the Winter Planet and had to be rescued. You have wasted my time and resources.' His hissing voice rises, 'The boy is gone with the girl twin, the Harlequin can't be found, the Demon seeks Willow endlessly, and you attempted to fight a force of Nature you have no understanding of. Do not let me down again. None of you will survive it.'

Magda Cross is livid to learn what has happened on Earth to her 'son', although she is not foolish enough to make any repost, her chances of surviving such an action would be minimal. A warning has been given. Typhon disappears, the Darkness hugs her, lifts her with whispers of undying love and affection, then they too are gone. Cravenclaw follows quickly.

The cat, an enormous ginger tomcat is silent, its every movement carefully placed as it creeps towards her. It settles itself ready to spring on the unsuspecting Willow, its talons extended. The excitement is too much. It sneezes twice in rapid succession, something that happens every time it gets close to a kill. Immediately the shocked Dormouse is running with a very frustrated Leeward in hot pursuit. He is destined to be disappointed as the little creature scuttles into a small hole. Although the cat sticks a paw into the hole she is out of reach. Leeward knows he does not have the time to wait out a siege on a mouse hole. His Master has need of him.

Willow could not transform back to human form without giving the game away, so she heaves a sigh of relief when she realises the cat has gone. She creeps slowly out of her hole.

Spellman, anxiously waiting for news on Alpha is mightily relieved to see her back. Together they hurry through the streets of Menos to find Rodrigo and Branca to warn them. They all then move quickly to give Adeth the news that Darius and Typhon are the same being. Immediately after hearing it he organises the Protectors to look for Darius but the traitor is nowhere to be found.

Adeth calls a meeting of the council assembly for the following day, while Rodrigo insists that Vivienne becomes the council leader's shadow. Branca stays close to Rodrigo, who as Ambrose's brother is bound to be a target while Spellman and Willow return to Earth.

36: AN EYE
FOR AN EYE

The picture messages from Ambrose are now getting weaker, the colours fading, the light diminishing. Rhea on the other hand is returning rapidly to full strength, fully believing her husband is still alive although very anxious about his health. While Rodrigo and his comrades are with Adeth, Chingis has arrived at the Fort. The magician/warrior is interested to find Harlequin there and watches him, he begins to wake up. Christine is helping him to sip some cool water from a flask. Jack suggests that one of the dragon sisters wipes Archie's memory. Lottie immediately disagrees with her brother,

'Not this time, I think. Where will he go? Where can we put him? I suggest we don't wake him yet until we speak to that one,' she points to Harlequin, 'it will help us decide what to do about him.'

She continues to say,

'We saw him walking with Archie and they

seem to have a good relationship. Meanwhile Mother,' she grins at Rhea, 'I think we should visit the house in Bristol and the one across the valley, sad as that will be, so you can see where we have been hidden all this time.'

'Yes,' her mother says smiling, 'that's a particularly good idea. You and Jack have heard a lot about your father but now I want to hear everything about you two.'

Spellman raises his head straight away and is about to protest. However, Chingis, recognising that Rhea needs some action and that it is especially important for the three of them to spend time together, holds his hand up to say,

'Lottie, I agree but you must take Spellman with you for protection, and you can't stay for too long I'm afraid.'

Spellman nods his head looking at Lottie who accepts the idea but asks where Willow is.

'She is with Eda.' Spellman replies.

Lottie pauses a moment then says,

'We shall be back here soon. Willow has been incredibly brave and it's time we talked. We cannot have Magda Cross driving a wedge between us.'

'Indeed,' is all Spellman says.

A little later Lottie and Jack wander together to the edge of the fort. The mountains roll in waves towards the coast, an ancient and sometimes mysterious landscape that holds it secrets well.

'We have found her, the first part is done, our Mother is safe,' Jack says turning to look at his sister.

'She is quite impressive isn't she,' Lottie grins while shielding her eyes from the sun.

'Yes,' he grins back. 'We have a lot to learn about each other which will be, I imagine, quite entertaining, particularly when we have found and rescued our father too.'

'Let's hope we are in time,' Lottie turns to him, the worry suddenly written all over her face.

'We will find him,' Jack says hugging his sister. Then looking at her his face set hard, 'We will find him.'

Several days later on a warm spring night, Jack and his mother are sitting on a bench in the communal garden opposite No 5 Maida Terrace in Bristol. The garden with its trees and shrubs is dimly lit by the streetlights on the road. It is a Saturday and Bristol City had been playing at home, they could all just about hear the roar of the crowd from the roof. Rhea, understanding the release it brings her son from more desperate things, is listening to Jack trying to explain to her the intricacies of the game of football.

Her eyes are shining, and she is smiling at him. Her happiness is mixed with an echoing sadness that washes over her from time to time as she thinks of all she has missed. However, she has realised the incredible changes her children have managed to get through together. Her belief that Ambrose is still alive, her determination to help them find him and bring him into their lives never falters.

It is beginning to get late. Jack stands up, yawns, and stretches,

'Time for bed I think.'

'Yes, I am tired too,' Rhea replies also standing up. 'Oh, there is another thing I wanted to ask you though. What are you going to do about Willow?'

Jack blushes slightly and is about to speak when there is a clicking noise. They both spin around, suddenly wide awake looking into the deep shadow in the corner of the garden. A group of party going students pass by whooping on down the road, and for the moment it is as though time is frozen. Then a frightening centipede like creature, a Tigari, moves out from the shadows to rear up saying in a clear quiet voice,

'I have come to speak to Lottie, my name is Florence. Tell her Menecapa returns his debt to her for saving his life with a message about the whereabouts of Ambrose.'

Meanwhile, Rodrigo is in the great hall in the City of Menos, at a council meeting where intense discussions are being held with plans being drawn up to deal with the gathering clouds of war. The discussions go on late into the evening. After a while as the talking comes to an end, he whispers to Branca,

'It looks as though we are done here for now. Spellman is back on Earth and I think I'll join him for a while.'

Branca moves to get up but Rodrigo says,

'It's OK, you needn't babysit me for this. I am going straight there and will then be in his and others company all the time. Bonny is also waiting for me to turn up.'

She nods her head as they clasp hands and he slips out of the great hall into the night.

Standing in the grounds, he gazes up at the stars lost in thought for a few moments unaware of a large ginger cat staring at him from the shadow of a tree. Seconds later the air shifts and he is confronted by Paedrenostra rising in front of him. A tall dark figure also quickly unravels. He can smell the putrid evil smelling breath as it washes over him, and a voice comes whispering loudly overtaking his mind saying,

'An eye for an eye Rodrigo, an eye for an eye.'

Later in the quiet and empty streets of Menos, the Darkness flows in the shadows, shivering with its black excitement, whispering like a soft evening breeze. It's creeping up walls, looking in at the windows, waiting for the time when the night grows still and the inhabitants have fallen asleep.

The End

ACKNOWLEDGE-MENT

I am grateful to family, friends and readers for their encouragement and critical interest which has helped to make this second book exist. I am particularly indebted to Sue Foot for reading and commenting on all the various drafts. To Alison Willows for her inciteful, close reading and for her expertise in translating its contents onto the promo video announcing the books arrival. Also, a huge thank you again to artist Nocola Latham for her comment and for again producing a superb original cover design. Belinda Febrey's enthusiasm and interest in continuing to act as an editor has been invaluable, helping to keep the book, indeed the series on track.

To my partner Anthea, a special thanks for her patience with the endless conversations, for her support and expertise in making the book work. Large parts of these books take place in Spain, especially Andalusia which we discovered during twenty years of visiting it on a motorcycle, and by continuing to live there for parts of the year.

Besides the aforementioned people, I am still inspired by the grandeur and mystery of the great Sierra Nevada in all its seasons, by the warmth and humour of the people, by the folklore and by flamenco. I wish I could dance.

Part of this book is also set in the City of Bristol, England which will always be for me, like coming back home.

Thank you for reading. I hope you are joining the journey to the story's conclusion a little further down the road.

ABOUT THE AUTHOR

Derek J Telling

Born in Bristol, England I 'came alive' in the heady days of the 1960's when anything seemed possible. Attempting a life as a poet, writer, musician (blowing the jug in a jug band!) I co-edited two poetry magazines, had several pieces of work published in well-known anthologies of the time, and a small volume by Driftwood Publications. I was one of the prime instigators of the Hydrogen Jukebox Show, a group of writers, actors and musicians performing in schools, colleges, festivals and pubs across the South West of England and beyond.

I began to realise after several years, that even in those gorgeous, challenging, and heady days, the funds to sustain a living were not going to fall into my lap so I turned to a full working life at the University of Bristol.

Eventually fully retiring from the University to live in Somerset and Andalucia, I have pursued a pathway of writing stories and songs (still attempting to play music but with a guitar!). Some of these have lain dormant for years.

My Grandmother taught me when I was very young and sitting around her winter fire, to read the stories in the hot and flaring embers. There were always dragons.

Contact us on

@derek.j.tellingbooks

djtbooks@gmail.com

BOOKS BY THIS AUTHOR

Brightest Light, Deepest Dark, Series

A Journey with Dragons and Dreams

Horizon. The Lost Planets

The following books in the series are currently in preparation for publication.

The Gatekeeper and the Coldfire Mirror

The Book of Impossible Deeds

Printed in Great Britain
by Amazon